Finding Home

Phetra H. Novak

Finding Home
Copyright © March 2016 by Phetra H. Novak

ISBN: 978 9 198295 86 3

Editor: Petra Howard
Cover Artist: Shayla Mist

Image/art disclaimer: Licensed material is being used for illustrative purposes only. Any person depicted in the licensed material is a model.

Published in the United States of America
Second Edition

* * * *

Warning:
This book contains sexually explicit scenes and adult language and may be considered offensive to some readers. This author's books are for sale to adults ONLY, as defined by the laws of the country in which you made your purchase.

ACKNOWLEDGMENTS

To all those who have to struggle to find a place they can call home, some never quite get there and are forever left searching. This is for them, too.

To my readers, thank you for taking the chance on a rookie and for staying faithful.

And always to my friends, family, and to all my Facebook friends, I cherish you every day. A special thanks to Hans for taking me under your wings for being real and for being a great friend.

Also a big thank you to Petra, Alp and Meg for helping with the dreaded editing in different stages of this book.

**The author acknowledges
the following brands or products:**

City of Gothenburg
Gothenburg University
Café Garbo
Varbergs Fästning – City of Varberg
Sahlgrenska University Hospital
Stetson – Hatco, Inc.
Stockholm Stock Exchange
Texas A & M University
Kindle – Amazon.com
Coke – The Coca-Cola Company
Goteborg Landvetter Airport – Swedavia
Espresso House – Goteborg Landvetter Airport, Swedavia
Chess Series by Sean Michael

TABLE OF CONTENTS

MEETING LUCA

TRAILING THE FLOW of students out of the lecture hall, Luca was deep in thought, still pondering the lecture he'd attended. Covering his mouth with his hand, he yawned discreetly; Dr. Larsson, from Sahlgrenska University Hospital, had given an interesting lecture about doctor-patient relationships, but it had been a long morning with only a short bathroom break. She had spent a lot of time giving examples of cases and had then invited everyone to practice in delivering difficult news, and how to do it without getting lost in the emotions.

"This is a balancing act, people. This will be your job; to help people who might be dying, and to find a way to tell them this without sounding coldhearted or bursting into tears. It will take time, practice, and a lot of trial and error. You will not be able to do this flawlessly first time around." She'd looked around at them, smiling. "Some of you are making the first mistake right now, looking at me, hearing what I say as a challenge, and deciding that you are going to prove me wrong and that you will be the one to manage this on the first try. Trust me when I say, you are the ones who will cry first."

A rumble of laughter had filled the lecture hall. Luca had smiled to himself, wondering if he would be the one.

Frowning, he stopped mid-stride, staring blindly at a spot in front of him. *Maybe I misunderstood? Did I completely miss what the lecturer wanted to say? No, no, of course not.* He'd been there and had participated in the discussion part; Dr. Larsson had even agreed with him on a point or two. *Hmm... Yes, she had.*

"Why bother with solving all that now," he mumbled to himself. "I am sure Father will have plenty to say about it later."

He let out a deep sigh, nodding to himself in agreement; it was exactly what would happen around the dinner table, as it did most days. He couldn't help but imagine what kind of man his father had been in his youth, especially since his uncle Soren was so very different. How many times in the last few years had he wished Soren and his wife Marie had been his parents? They didn't see them often because, according to his father, Soren was a traitor.

Soren had told him a few things over the years, during the times when they'd been able to talk to each other privately. The last time Luca had seen his uncle had been nearly two years ago when his grandfather had died. They did talk on the phone from time to time, usually when his uncle called him to make sure he was doing okay and to see generally how things were going. He recalled his uncle's words from their last conversation, which had been several weeks ago.

"Luca, you have a choice here, you know this, right? It isn't like we live at the end of the world and your dad is the king. What's the worst thing that can happen?"

"He'll be disappointed in me if I quit, and my life will be a living hell in that house with him."

Luca had answered immediately but, in all honesty, he wasn't entirely sure how his father would react. His father, Anders, had never hit him, yet somewhere in his gut was a feeling that it would not be out of his comfort zone to do so.

That was why he never really put up a fight. He'd known all his life that this was the route he was expected to take. He'd never questioned his parents' wishes—not once. Training to be a vet? Off the table. But animals were so much easier to deal with. They were less complicated and a lot friendlier. His forehead wrinkled, thinking about his father and "the master plan." As always, his stomach knotted when he thought of the brilliant surgeon, Dr. Anders Von Bergendahl; he knew that he'd never fill those shoes for the sole reason he didn't have his father's cold mindset or the sharp elbows.

Luca was abruptly brought out of his thoughts when someone rammed him from behind and sent him flying. He barely managed to stay on his feet and threw out an arm to grab hold of the railing in an attempt to stop himself falling. The chump who'd almost knocked him over went tearing down the stairs, running for dear life, but he was laughing—yelling out a petty "sorry" as he disappeared down the road, chased by another.

"Are you all right?"

Luca snapped his head around; he hadn't heard the stranger approach. His hand was on his arm and helped him stand up straight.

"That was a nasty shove you got there. What an asshole. You feeling okay?" The stranger gave Luca a friendly smile.

Clearing his throat, Luca could feel his cheeks warming in embarrassment but he smiled back.

"Yes...yes...thank you," he whispered.

Looking around, he realized the incident has stirred attention. Feeling his cheeks heat up even more, he mumbled a thank-you to the stranger and practically ran down the stairs to get away.

Oh God! Oh God! Why does this always happen to me! Hurrying along, keeping his head down, he avoided the curious looks of the people he passed, wanting to get away as quickly as possible. He cut across the grass to the sidewalk beside the main road of Vasagatan. After a block, he slowed his pace, feeling he was far enough away from Gothenburg University and all those people.

"Why is fate always playing these mean jokes on me?"

3

He hefted his bookbag over his shoulder once more before pressing the back of his hand to his flaming cheeks. Taking a look around, he let out a shaky breath of relief when he realized no one was watching him.

Three whole days cooped up in a lecture hall was tough on him. It was too crowded and, no matter how hard he tried, large groups of people made him nervous. When he had to spend time with people his own age, he always felt queasy. Never fitting in, always the odd man out. That was the reason he mostly spent his time alone, and when not studying, he read voraciously.

According to his mother, it was because he "didn't try hard enough." Luca could hear her voice ringing in his head, telling him to "be more sociable," as if it was an internal switch he could flip to the "on" position, and it would make people like him or he'd feel less awkward around them.

Luca's mother loved people, new and existing. She loved talking and socializing, his father less so but, when he had to, he did it well.

While everyone else was so sure about who they were and what they wanted to do, Luca had no idea whatsoever. Well, he did, but it wasn't like he could talk his parents about it. He could imagine that conversation.

"No; what I really want to be is a veterinarian."

"So why are you studying to become a doctor?"

"Because my father said so."

For Luca, it was all about doing what kept other people happy and kept him out of the spotlight. That had been a great plan until his last year of secondary school when reality caught up and he found himself no longer in the comfort of the basic school system. Instead, he had to start on the path down a road he really didn't care for and pay careful attention to what his father said.

Of course, he wasn't a puppet, but keeping up appearances was important; that, mostly, came from his mother. His parents were a well-oiled machine that crushed his childhood notions of becoming a vet, and these days, with so many restrictions, he felt more and more awkward. Who else, aged twenty, had to endure the Spanish Inquisition over a simple party invitation?

A moped passed by him, making him jump in fright. Clasping a hand to his chest, he chuckled to himself. "I really need to stop living inside my head!"

Securing his bookbag on his shoulder—again—he made himself slow down as he scuttled along Vasa Street to catch his tram home. His stomach grumbled loudly and, with a quick glance at his watch, he realized how many hours it had been since breakfast. His phone buzzed in his jeans pocket; retrieving it, he glanced at the display. *Great! Just what I needed…not!*

"Hello, Father," he said matter of fact.

"You sound off? Where are you?"

No "Hello, how are you?" Straight to the point, as always.

"Downtown still. The lecture just ended a little bit ago."

"But it was supposed to have ended at noon. What have you been doing between now and then?"

"Dad, the lecture ended like fifteen minutes ago. You can call the department head and check if you don't believe me."

"Luca, really. I asked you a simple question. Why does everything have to become an issue with you?"

Luca shook his head, rolling his eyes. "Sorry."

"Okay. I've been invited to a dinner to meet a group of surgeons, which I cannot say no to. I won't be home until later this evening. Are you done with your studies?"

"Yes, all of them."

"Good. Then it doesn't matter to me what you do for the rest of the day. But I expect you to be home by the time I get back, which should be by eleven p.m. at the latest."

Holy shit! Was his father giving him an afternoon and an evening off? Telling him to have fun? Luca took a second to check his phone to make sure it was, in fact, his father's number on the screen.

"Thanks, Dad. I'll stay downtown and go grab some lunch."

"Fine. Don't do anything stupid, and call and leave a message on my cell so I know what you're doing."

"Okay, sure."

Whatever; he was going to have an afternoon off. Why go home when he could stay here and enjoy himself a little? Maybe he could go to one of his favorite cafés. The weather was warm enough so he could sit outside, read and watch people. The idea made him smile. *I can splurge on this. I've done my work this week and it is, after all, Friday.*

With a bounce back in his step and humming to himself, the tension slowly eased its way out of his body. All thoughts about his father—the knot-maker—pushed out of his mind, at least for the moment.

Feeling a lot better about things, he set off toward one of his favorite cafés: Garbo.

His father was such an odd man; Luca had a hard time relating to him. But, hardship or not, he wasn't going to look a gift horse in the mouth by questioning where this sudden good grace from his father had come from. He was free for the rest of the afternoon. He was lucky that learning came easy to him, and he didn't have to study that hard. That also kept his scores and knowledge high, which, in turn, kept his father's nagging to a minimum.

His father loved pop-quizzing him, and Luca was sure the demands made of him were much more than other students got from their parents.

Luca, it isn't about passing. It is about becoming the leading surgeon in the country. You are not some medical student; you are a Von Bergendahl. Luca had heard the speech so many times he knew it by heart.

The sun was shining down, warming him, making it comfortable to go without his jacket, so he shrugged out of it, shoved it in his backpack, and turned his face up towards the sun like a hibernating animal that had awoken for spring. It was one of his favorite things about animals, watching them as they woke up from the long sleep of winter. Like cows, for instance: they were housed inside for the winter, and the first time they walked out to a green-covered-meadow, the sun warm on their hides, those large, heavy creatures would jump and kick into the air as if they were light as a feather. Their emotions were always genuine and easy to interpret.

Luca smiled to himself. Of all farm animals, he loved cows the best. They were large but gentle animals, affectionate, too. Cows weren't meant to be inside, but it didn't hurt them if they had enough space, and they needed to be protected from the harsh elements of winter. Sweden, thank God, had great laws to prevent animals from being mistreated.

If he could only do as he pleased and become a veterinarian, he'd move out into the country and have a classic country practice.

Imagine how happy I'd be. A house in the country, a few dogs, maybe a cat, and a library full of books. Yes! Yes! Catching himself daydreaming about things that would never be, he quickly shut himself off; he'd almost shouted that last "yes" out loud.

There was no point in daydreaming about such things. It would only make his life that much harder, not easier.

Almost at Garbo Café, he passed a few of his fellow students. On any given day, he'd walk on by with his head down to avoid the possibility of meeting people he barely knew, since he never spoke to them unless it was in class.

With eye contact came interaction, and he sucked at casual conversation.

Synergy with peers led to conversation, which led to questions—questions he didn't know how to answer. It made him uncomfortable, feeling as if people could see things he didn't want them to see.

But today, he was caught up in his own world and met a couple of their gazes head-on, giving them a bright smile and a light wave before he could stop himself. A girl waved back.

"Luca!" She called after him, making him slow down even if he didn't stop completely. "Come over here and let me introduce you to some of my friends."

He shook his head instantly. "I'm sorry, I can't. I'm busy."

She stood up and headed towards him. What did she want? Hadn't he said he was busy? Before he could collect himself enough to walk off, she was there, taking his hand, pulling him towards the group of girls.

"But, I… I have to go, please." Luca dug his heels in yet somehow ended up next to the other girls sitting on the park bench, chatting away.

"Ladies, this is Luca, the guy I told you about. We're in the same biochemistry class." The four girls smiled, one giggled, and looked at him from under her lashes. Was she flirting with him?

"You were right, Stina, he is cute," one of them said. Were they talking about him? Luca could feel his face turning warm. He opened his mouth to say something, anything, but nothing came out.

"Isn't he, though?" Stina smiled, bumping his shoulder. "Josefine here thinks you're cute. Maybe you could buy her a cup of coffee sometime," she suggested easily, all of them looking at him, waiting for him to say something.

"Oh, look how adorable, he's blushing." Luca closed his eyes; he had to get out of there. *Now!*

"Girls, be nice." Stina protested, but there was no sternness to her voice. Instead, it made the other girls chuckle more, and their gazes seemed to get even more intense.

"So, what has you so busy on a Friday that you can't hang with us?" Stina asked, looking directly at him, hands on her hips.

"I'm sorry, I have to go. It was nice meeting you," he managed before hurrying off.

He felt ridiculous, running off like a little kid. *Again.* But, it was too late now; it wasn't as if he could turn around and say, "Oh, by the way…"

There were times he wondered if it was his parents' pressuring that made him so uptight. He didn't have to wonder: it *was* the pressure from his parents that made him act like a lunatic when someone tried to engage him in conversation. It was annoying as hell, reacting like he did because a girl flirted with him. But, in the moment, he couldn't stop himself. It wasn't until he calmed down that he'd realize how much of a drama queen he'd been. The worst thing with girls who seemed intent on him was the flirting—batting their eyelashes at him, or touching his arm to get his attention. How the hell did you respond to it when you weren't interested?

Jessica, the only friend he had—who, funnily enough, was a girl—said the butterflies were supposed to come all by themselves, making you act all silly and flirty without having to think about it. It didn't happen for him, ever. She always told him to relax.

Be yourself, Luca. You're a good-looking guy, and you have interesting things to say. You need to relax a little, and not assume the worst about people. Then she would give him one of her radiant smiles and start talking about something else.

Walking down the stairs leading to Garbo Café, he ducked through the low-situated doorway of the café and immediately got in line to order.

Glancing up at the chalkboard hanging above the cash register, he started to look over the menu. He was hungry—like, starving—and needed something filling. There were plenty of things to choose from, but it didn't take him long to pick the chicken pie that came with a garden salad, as it was something he seldom ate at home. Quiche, which, in his world, was the same thing as pie, was fine to serve, but pie, no—that was devil's food. He much preferred Swedish husmanskost—home cooking—than fine dining. But, of course, in his house, that was too plain.

The food served at home was like one of his mother's dinner parties: stiff and boring. The thought of one of those parties made Luca wrinkle his nose in dismay. He hated those rich man's parties. Not only were they unimaginative and a hoax, the people attending them were mostly fake and tedious, too. They came because it was expected. That was probably a slight exaggeration—fine, a huge exaggeration—but he wasn't a fan.

There could be twenty or so people invited to one of these parties, a "small gathering" according to his mother. The conversation would be polite and restricted to speaking inanely about the weather, hobbies, their newest purchases, or something else equally neutral.

There would be no political, religious, or sexual orientation discussions. Gossip was allowed. And, whatever you did, no cracking a joke. God forbid you actually had fun. Everything was kept in neat little boxes, and anything that wasn't considered acceptable, they pretended didn't exist. In twenty years, that would be him and the wife he'd been told to marry.

Oh, my god! I'm becoming my parents.

He *was* becoming them, slowly but surely. In twenty years or so, he'd be this hard and bitter man with a wife, kids, and a damn Volvo. He wouldn't be happy, but he'd be a surgeon, and that was all that mattered to his parents. But not to him, not at all, and he had to do something to stop it.

He had to start taking some risks, even if they seemed like small ones to anyone else. If he didn't, the upcoming years of university would become even longer, lonelier, and—foremost—duller than ever. It didn't take a genius to know his behavior today wasn't normal in any sense of the word.

He couldn't let himself be ruled by the fear of having to deal with his father and what he might do if Luca did something he didn't agree with. He wasn't a bad person; he didn't do awful things. Luca refused to believe his father would truly hurt him. He had to start living more for himself than to please his parents. He might not get all the things he wanted for himself, but he'd be damned if he let someone else control every aspect of his life.

Baby steps.

THE MEETING

KAI SAW THE object of his obsession leaving the lecture hall and stroll towards one of the small cafés he'd seen him at a couple of times. It was where he'd first laid eyes on him, over three weeks ago. Sometimes, Luca went in to buy a coffee on his way to class. Often, Kai knew he'd stay there for hours, slaving over his books, and observe. He never sat or walked with anyone, always alone. It broke Kai's heart a little each time but it made his affection for him increase, and the urge to make contact even greater.

Kai couldn't imagine how it was to always be that alone. Most of his life he'd been surrounded by family and friends, and he loved that. So, when he noticed Luca he immediately wanted to become his friend. If he admitted it to himself, which he did easily, his interest went beyond wanting to be friends. He was attracted to him like crazy. However, unlike him Luca was shy; Kai knew approaching him would have to be done with care.

Kai followed at a safe distance as he didn't want to be caught, at least not until he was ready to be seen. Today he was making his move, he was going to introduce himself but it needed to be at the right moment.

Kai had been in Gothenburg, Sweden, for almost four months and loved it. He missed home but it had been the right decision to go to Europe for a semester and get the experience. It would be something he'd never forget. The Swedes, in general, were mostly open-minded people and friendly, and the country itself was gorgeous—so different from back home. Nearly everyone spoke English really well, so, even though he was away from home, he still had the comfort of making himself understood. It was great. He was majoring in agriculture and only had his thesis left. Writing had always come easily to him, so being here wasn't a hardship.

He'd been fascinated and completely taken off balance the first time he'd seen the Swede. He assumed he was; he had that look to him. There was something fresh faced and healthy looking about the Scandinavians. All Swedes seemed to be quite a bit taller than the average American. Luca had well sculpted but not I-go-to-the-gym-and-lift-weights-six-times-a-week leg muscles, a fit body, and a nice set of shoulders.

Kai wasn't the least bit vain, but he'd often been told how good looking he was. Girls asked him if he really was gay, and some were put off when he answered yes. Some truly thought it was him blowing them off, even though he was never seen around town with any girls, at least not in a way that could be interpreted as dating. Personally he didn't think he was that special in the looks department, it was the fact that he wasn't available at all for some that made him shine extra bright to some. Luca on the other hand was stunning.

Watching the handsome Swede, he could appreciate the physical attraction, too, even if he was built nothing like him.

He was at least a couple of inches taller than him. His legs seemed to go on forever. The sweet bubble butt, which put a slight curve in the long, lean runner's body, looked good enough to make any man walk right up and cup those globes purely to cop a feel. The narrow waist and torso matched the rest of his lean physique. It was easy to say he was every gay cowboy's version of a Swedish Bikini, or—in this case—Speedo team.

The day he first saw him, Kai had been in a hurry to meet his friends for a late lunch but he'd stopped dead in his tracks as this absolutely gorgeous person appeared before him. He'd been so taken aback; he'd been locked in place right there on the open street, ogling.

Luca was an odd mix of ravishing and, for lack of a better word, beautiful. Large blue eyes—the same color as the ocean—with eyelashes so dark and full that, when he looked at you, it almost felt like you were drowning. He'd been lost. Luca's blond curls were wild and untamable and gave him an innocent look. They framed his delicate face accenting his high, defined cheekbones in a way that made you hold your breath. And the way he moved...at least, when he didn't think anyone was watching! It was easy, almost like he was gliding. The smile that usually painted his face when he looked like he was busy daydreaming made his entire face light up.

When Kai had finally been able to collect himself enough to go on, he'd been happy he was in an open-minded country like Sweden. Ogling as he'd done wouldn't have flown—no matter the gender but especially not same sex—if he'd been in Texas.

Kai thought Luca had this odd but adorable behavior about him. He walked around almost lost in his own thoughts, talking to himself, not loud enough so it made him weird but he seemed completely unaware of the world going on around him. His behavior wasn't overly odd, merely enough to make him stand out, and in Kai's eyes become even more appealing. He was always so wrapped up in his own thoughts he'd never once noticed Kai watching him.

Kai had started to feel dumb, stalking Luca without introducing himself. But he hadn't been able to help himself, he'd been so much fun to watch. He was taking his time to make contact since he seemed skittish, almost scared to talk to people. Kai had watched him avoid people he knew several times, even when he seemed to want to reach out and talk to them. It was enough to make Kai wary on how to approach him without scaring him off or making too much of a fool of himself.

To Kai it was fascinating that someone so absolutely stunning seemed to be so unaware of the draw he had on people.

Kai wasn't anything like that. Growing up on a ranch in Texas with an older brother, younger sister, and his parents, he'd learned from an early age to make himself be seen. His brother Kit was only a year older than him, and they were close. In some ways, he was Kai's best friend and, all through life, they shared practically everything. The same thing went for his dad. His pops was, to put it mildly, the best damn dad anyone could have, always supportive, always there with time to listen. Kai loved his family and they returned the love.

Being gay had never been an issue to them; he'd had a good life and still did. Coming to Sweden to study had actually been his father's idea. He wanted him to know for sure what he wanted to do with his life, not merely settle for the ranch without knowing what else was out there. Through his school, he'd found this exchange program and had happily come to the home of the smorgasbords and beautiful blonds. And Luca in particular.

He guessed—if he was going to be honest, which he tried to be as a rule—if he had a type, he usually went for jocks. Big, well-defined, types of jocks who liked it a bit rough. Smiling to himself, he could see the look on his family and friends' faces when they found out he was infatuated with someone like Luca, who was quite the opposite to his usual type. But Kai thought he was breathtaking and beautiful— watching him made him smile.

Besides, Kai hadn't chosen him, it was the other way around.

From the moment he'd seen him, he'd been hooked and wanted to find out more about him. Luca wasn't like any of the others. The often repeated and misquoted, "I just want to be left alone," by Greta Garbo, reminded Kai of the object of his obsession who preoccupied his mind more than anything or anyone at the moment. It was apt that this café seemed to be a favorite of his.

Kai watched as he crossed the street and walked down the narrow stairs into the coffee shop. It was time and he didn't want to let another opportunity pass him by. His friends, when he asked them about Luca, didn't know much but Axel had told him Luca's name, and that he'd seen Luca participate in a large discussion during a seminar. It was easy to see Luca had been confident and outspoken but, as soon as it was over and time to mingle, he'd pulled away and walked off on his own.

This could have been mistaken for arrogance but one of the first things that made Kai aware of him had been the sad look in his eyes when he thought no one was looking. He always smiled and talked politely with people but when he was alone, the sadness would cloud his eyes again.

All of Kai's instincts had made him want to take Luca into his arms and hug him till the sadness went away. He'd been so completely captivated by him that he couldn't stay away, and that in itself was something new for Kai to experience.

Back home in Texas, Kai was never without a date or roll in the hay if that was what he wanted. Not that he cared about that, because the most important people in Kai's life, besides his parents, were his friends. Kai was damn well aware of how lucky he was to have such great people around him. They never once judged him and always had his back.

Living in Texas wasn't exactly the gay man's number one paradise, but it was home.

Kai let a tram pass before he crossed the street and half ran up on the sidewalk. He steered himself after Luca and toward Garbo. Kai actually felt nervous about approaching him, but he couldn't keep creeping around in the bushes any longer. If Luca ever found out, he'd most likely be weirded out and, to be honest, Kai was kind of creeping himself out.

It had always been easy for Kai to make new friends and first contact. He enjoyed talking with, and meeting, new people, but this was quite different. His interest in Luca was personal—very personal—he was more attracted to him than he should be, since he'd never even talked to him. But, he couldn't deny the stir of emotions or the massive amount of butterflies fluttering in his stomach every time he saw him or even thought about him.

By pure accident, he'd bumped into him once outside class. He'd been lucky and caught Luca on one of those rare occasions where he'd actually stayed behind to talk to people. Kai couldn't remember what they'd been talking about or if he'd even heard any of the conversation because Luca had smiled, and it had changed everything.

One of his favorite things about observing him was seeing those smiles of pure joy. They never lasted long but his face became alive. Then, all too soon, he'd pull back into his shell. It was as if he realized he was living and had to stop himself. You could tell from a mile away that Luca felt insecure with attention if it ever surrounded him. There had been numerous times when Kai had to restrain himself to not walk right up to Luca and rescue him, like some damn idiot with a "knight in shining armor" complex. But the desire had been there from the first day. Whatever urges Kai had, he'd resisted them, so he could find one perfect moment to make Luca's acquaintance.

Entering the small café, Kai took off his baseball cap. Leaving the Stetson off was hard enough; not having a hat at all was a no-go. Spinning his hat in his hand, exactly like he'd do with his Stetson, he let his eyes adapt to the dimmed light. He quickly searched for the object of his affection, his lips curling into a soft smile when he saw Luca by the register. He was fumbling with his backpack; it insisted on gliding down his arm as he struggled to pick up his utensils. Kai's smile got even wider, watching him, and he took a few steps forwards to introduce himself and be the gentleman his momma raised him to be.

* * * *

Feeling less panicked over his current epiphany about becoming like his father, Luca realized he was next in line to order. Taking the few steps closer to the counter, he had to make a decision on lunch. He chuckled at his own indecisions but, in his defense, Garbo's meat pie selection was legendary.

They always had several different kinds. Today it was spicy Mexican minced meat and broccoli pie, ham and cheese, and a Greek pie with feta cheese and olives. He licked his lips, eyeing the pies, all encased in buttery, flaky pastry. His eyes wandered over the big selection of gourmet sandwiches. The choice of the day was lasagna and a sandwich cake.

He wrinkled his nose—sandwich cake was a misnomer; it was topped with different kinds of potted herring. How people could eat that was beyond him and he was a Swede. He was supposed to like cold, raw fish. Using a type of Swedish flatbread—a little thicker than normal flatbread—the filling wasn't too bad, it was usually sour cream mixed with garlic, red onion, and some of the juice from the herring. However, the nasty mustard or tomato sauce covered cold fish—they were disgusting. An involuntary shiver rippled through him. He shuddered. *Yuck!*

Finally, his turn, he bit his lip as he made a snap decision. He ordered the homemade minced meat pie, instead of the original chicken he'd had in mind, with a side order from the salad buffet, and a large latte. As he paid, his book bag slid down his arm again. Why was he even surprised? He was so preoccupied with trying to grab his coffee and food, as well as getting his bag under control, that he didn't notice the person standing behind him until he turned around and slammed right into him, spilling coffee all over the floor and the stranger's hands.

For a moment, all he could do was stand there, staring at the coffee dripping off the man's hands.

Oh, please! Please! Pleeease… Don't let this be happening to me. No more.

He squeezed his eyes shut as he silently begged for him to be gone when he opened them again, but he wasn't that fortunate. The only thing he was grateful for was that his damn book bag had slid down between them; otherwise, he would've had coffee all over his massive chest. Luca fumbled to place his items back on the counter, and tried to grab for some napkins. The girl behind the counter helped him out by handing him a towel and a small ice pack for the bloke's hands.

"Hell, I'm so sorry! Did you burn yourself? I'm such a klutz." He babbled as he let his backpack slide off his shoulder and drop to the floor by his feet. Of course, all the stuff from his bag conveniently slipped out, spreading across the floor in front of them. He sighed internally, rolling his eyes. This was his typical felicity; he couldn't seem to catch a break.

Luca reached for the stranger's hands, drying them off quickly, taking a good look to make sure he hadn't burnt him. Because of his father, he had a little more knowledge than most pre-med students when it came to basic medicine, his father had made sure of that. So, he knew what he was supposed to be looking for but didn't find any serious damage on either of his hands. A couple of spots were a little red and might sting for a bit, but they should be better in a couple hours.

He applied the icepack to the red spots on the hand. "I can't begin to express how sorry I am. I'm clumsy. I'm so sorry!"

How could I have been this careless? Sure, I'm a little stressed out, the pressure of always having to be perfect affects me but still, I'm not usually this much of a mess. What the hell is wrong with me?

Realizing he hadn't been paying attention to the man standing in front of him, Luca looked at his hands, which he was still holding on to. He let them go instantly. *Jesus! Could this day get any weirder!*

"Are you okay? How are your hands? Do you want me to take another look? I'm a medical student." He grabbed one hand again for another inspection, then snapped his mouth closed as he realized he was babbling. *Come on, where the hell had that come from? Like it mattered. What did being a medical student have to do with anything? He must think I'm a complete moron with no self-control.*

Luca heard him chuckle and forced himself to stop his internal scolding to look up and meet his eyes. The world came to a sudden halt, as did Luca's breath.

"Oh." The word wasn't any louder than the softest whisper. The most amazing brown eyes he'd ever seen mesmerized Luca. They were a deep, warm, golden brown and, when you looked into them, it was as if they were smiling. For several moments he stood there with the stranger's hand in his, staring into them, forgetting everything else. Luca couldn't say for how long he stood there, as time faded away. It could have been anywhere from one minute to an hour. Not until he cleared his throat and Luca felt the touch of his hand on his arm, did he finally snap out of his daze.

He was mesmerized when he looked down at the large heavy hand on his arm and back up into those eyes, still taken aback and slightly shocked by his own reaction. He'd been caught staring. As if on cue, Luca blushed bright-red from embarrassment. He wanted nothing more than the earth to open up and swallow him whole.

His eyes flickered to his feet and the mess on the floor. *I have to get out of here before I make an even bigger ass of myself than I already have.* Taking the opportunity to not look back up, Luca bent down to get his backpack and started to shove things back into it, mumbling to himself what a complete dumb-ass he was making of himself.

THE COFFEE HAD been hot as it ran over his hands but Kai was too preoccupied watching Luca to notice much. Besides, it was worth the small ache to have Luca touch him. It was like an electric current zinging through his hands. He smiled as Luca started to speak quickly, apologizing. Kai had picked up enough Swedish over the past months to understand the major things he was saying. And, whatever he missed, he didn't bother trying to decipher in his head. listening to his voice was good enough for him. He was adorable in the cutest guyish way a man his age could be.

He hadn't had a thing for so-called pretty boys like Luca in the past but he was completely and utterly sold on this one. Reaching out, trying to get Luca to stop and see him, their eyes locked for the first time and everything around them went quiet. He could feel the connection between them. Luca must have felt it, too, if the look on his face was anything to go by. Kai knew he was right.

The moment lasted longer than he thought Luca would let it but, in his defense, Kai thought he was probably a little shocked, not only because he'd been startled as he bumped into him but also with the thing passing between them. He couldn't help smiling. If his brother had been there, he would have taken him aside and told him to pull on the reins, hold his horses. Back off a bit, let things take their course and not rush or push things too much. His brother Kit always said he was very much like their sister when it came to pushing too much, too soon.

Kai knew Kit was right, not that he'd tell him that, but Kai saw something and then, bam, he decided right then and there what he thought. After he'd made up his mind, it took something huge to make him change his point of view. Luca was like that to him. Knowing him or not, the minute he'd seen him, he knew he wanted him. All he could do now was pray for fate to be good to him, and make sure he was as gay as he was.

"Let me help you," Kai said, hunching down, his knees cracking. Luca jumped a little as he spoke, dropping the book he'd only recently picked up. Kai knew his voice was quite deep but he didn't think that was why Luca had reacted the way he had. A shiver went through Luca's body when his fingers grazed Kai's as they reached for the same book making his skin prickle at the simple and soft touch.

"YOU'RE AN AMERICAN." His voice was barely audible. "I'm so sorry, I didn't know…or I would have spoken to you in English. Are you all right? I'm awfully sorry," he said again, stammering a little, looking into the pretty man's eyes.

Pretty? Jeez, where did that come from? Luca let himself look a little closer; he was handsome with dimples and kind eyes. *That's okay, right? It's facts. Anyone could see he was handsome and would agree with him.* He felt himself smiling back, being drawn in deeper, and it was such an easy thing to do.

23

He couldn't stop looking. It wasn't until the skin on his hand felt like it was being charged with tiny electrical pulses that he looked away. He gasped, his fingers twitching from the light touch of this stranger's hand slipping on top of his. He didn't know what to do with the odd feeling starting in the pit of his stomach and slowly moving like a wave of warmth through his entire body.

"I'm fine, it aches a little, but I'll live. I startled you, so it's my own fault." He smiled and Luca matched it with one of his own. "And you apologize way too much. No need."

He picked up the last book, placing it gently back into his book bag. It gave Luca a chance to look away because he could feel his cheeks heating in embarrassment. He always did that, apologize for everything and blush furiously, too, when he thought about it. He had the worst poker face ever, his face was like an open book, and he knew it.

"It's all good," he said, most likely to reassure him again.

"I can be such a klutz sometimes, today isn't my day. To be honest, I've felt like this humongous dumbass all day, failing miserably at living," Luca said with a laugh, trying to lighten the sudden tension with a joke.

He was blushing again, he hated it that it was so easy for him to do, but blushing he did, always and often. Pretending nothing of it Luca kept his eyes on the bloke before him.

"Not a dumbass at all. From my where I'm standing, it looks like a mighty fine ass to me." He joked, making Luca mouth fall open for a second. He swallowed hard, blushing even more. *Oh, for the love of God can I stop with the blushing already! I should have stayed in bed today. I realize this now.*

Luca's sighed, dropping his gaze immediately, looking at a very interesting spot on the floor but couldn't help studying the coffee guy from under his eyelashes. Luca couldn't help to wonder why he was still standing there, it was as if he wanted to say and talk to him.

What was even more amazing was that Luca didn't mind, he was fascinated and would like to talk to him a little more. There was something about him that made Luca want to find out more about him. From the look of things, coffee guy was observing him as much as Luca was observing him.

Luca was having a hard time breathing, his breath had been stolen from him. Good God, why was he so nervous? Shaken. He was weak in the knees, for crying out loud. If this guy didn't stop watching him, he'd have to run away screaming. Sliding his gaze over him, taking in his entire form, Luca thought it would help to focus his eyes. On the contrary, his pulse sped up to where he thought it was going to beat a hole through his chest. The way the man's jeans molded onto his hips and thighs, you'd think someone had sewn them on him. It was as if he'd walked out of one of those girls' magazines where there was always some sexy mystery man on the cover. Not that he'd worked hard to notice, of course; it was obvious.

Luca's tongue flicked out to lick his suddenly dry lips, studying the American man's face. High cheekbones, full lips, hair curling around his ears. Unable to resist the urge, he had to let his eyes roam over his strong body again. Eventually, Luca forced himself to look away, scolding himself. *This is starting to become utterly ridiculous! If I didn't know better I'd say I was standing here eyeing him up, like I was actually attracted to him. Which I'm not...right? Of course not, I like girls, not any of the girls I've met so far.*

"There you go, it's all back in there." The stranger stood up, holding his bookbag out. Luca took it, still a little shaky and his heart beat slightly too irregularly. But he took a deep breath and smiled.

"Thank you and I'm awfully sorry for all of this." He rolled his eyes inwardly, how many times was he going to repeat himself? He should have gone home right after the lecture. This obviously wasn't going to be one of his better days.

"That's okay. No harm, no foul." His smile grew wider, showing off a dimple in his right cheek. He opened his mouth to speak again, Luca was sure it was to say goodbye and leave but he couldn't let that happen.

Before he could stop himself, he blurted out, "Please, let me buy you lunch as a thank you for being such a good sport and helping my fumbling bum out. I insist." Luca's eyelids closed abruptly in a reflex reaction. Oh God, he could have kicked himself for that comment. He didn't ask strangers to have lunch with him but he just had. This had to be what possession by aliens felt like. There was no other explanation for the awkward mess he was making.

"You have a very expressive face. Everything you're thinking shows like a silent movie. It's fun. I like it. You shouldn't be so hard on yourself. You're doing fine, and as for the spilt coffee, that should teach me not to sneak up on people." He smiled and held out a hand. "I'm Kai, Kai Kelly."

Taking his outstretched hand, Luca returned his friendly smile. If the Kai hadn't left by now, he probably wasn't going to and it couldn't get any worse than this. No way. He took Kai's hand and shook it. The warmth of his skin made his body tingle again but, for once, Luca managed to keep his reaction hidden. At least he thought he had. "I'm Luca. It's very nice to meet you, Kai."

"It's very nice to meet you, too, Luca. If you meant what you said about joining you for lunch, don't mind if I do. I'm starving."

CANDLELIGHT

KAI HAD NEVER been so grateful to have coffee poured over him as he was today. Luca insisted on paying for lunch. He didn't agree that he had to but he knew Luca felt guilty, and let him treat him for lunch. They took their meals to a quiet corner on the outside terrace at one of the tables with the wooden chairs and basket-like seats.

At first, Kai had to carry out most of the conversation, which he was happy to. He wanted to show Luca he wasn't a bad person, and to help him relax. Luca helped by laughing at his lame attempts at jokes, and asking the occasional question. Mostly, those pretty, blue eyes focused on him. It felt good to be the focus of those amazing blues and it gave him the impression Luca was interested in him and very much part of the conversation, even if he didn't say much at first.

He sat, silent for a moment, watching Luca pick at his salad. Kai was fascinated by what he'd put on his plate. It seemed to be all meats and cheeses salad and pie. It was nothing like a salad back home at all. There were thick slices of feta cheese, red onion, and various dressings. Eventually, Luca started to relax and share things about himself. Even though he'd warmed up to Kai, he was still cautious and reserved as if he was trying hard to act accordingly. The last thing Kai wanted to do was scare him away.

Their food got eaten all to fast and when it was long gone and then some, Kai wanted to convince Luca to go and have a few beers. He wasn't ready to say goodbye yet.

"Come on, let's grab a couple beers somewhere." He smiled, nudging Luca's arm playfully. "It's Friday, still early, and we've got so much to talk about. I'd really like to get to know you more. Come, spend some time with me." Luca watched him like he'd given him the moon. Kai wondered if anyone ever gave this sweet man the time of day. He couldn't understand why anyone wouldn't have time for someone like him.

"Oh… I… Okay. Let me text my parents to let them know I'll be home a little later than expected." Luca cleared his throat, and added. "They're such worrywarts."

"No problem. Now you can take me to your favorite place."

Luca texted with quick fingers but lifted his gaze every few seconds to show he was still paying attention to what Kai was saying.

"So you being a native and all, where do we go? You have a favorite pub?"

"I'm sorry," he said so softly Kai barely heard him, "I'll have to crawl to the cross on that one."

Kai laughed. "What does that mean?"

"It's a Swedish saying. It means to admit one was wrong or to have a lack of knowledge on something you should have known. For me, I'm embarrassed to say I have no idea where to go because I never go out, like ever. I don't have a favorite pub. I'm one of those boring people who doesn't get out much." He shrugged, looking down at his feet, Kai had noticed he always did it when he was embarrassed.

"Hey." Kai put a finger under Luca's chin tipping it up until their eyes met. "None of that, okay? No beating yourself up. Your city is full of bars; I'd say you have more bars per capita than Bryan, Texas." He smiled, hoping his confidence rubbed off on Luca, he wanted him to feel comfortable and happy to be there with him, just like Kai felt being there with Luca.

Kai reluctantly let go of Luca's chin. What he really wanted to do was keep staring into those blue eyes and maybe, entirely maybe, have a taste of those pretty lips. But he didn't. This was not the time or place to do that. He wasn't even sure Luca wanted that.

"Maybe not pubs, but cafés for sure. Did you know that Gothenburg has the most cafés per capita in Europe?"

"No. I didn't know that."

"We do. We drink a lot of hot beverages. Interesting facts about Gothenburg. Not. As you Americans say," Luca said with an embarrassed, crooked-looking smile.

"Must be the freezing weather, and all the polar bears in the streets doing that." Kai teased Luca, glad when his eyes sparkled.

Snorting, Luca glared at him playfully. "Yeah, the polar bears would do it. Do people actually believe that about here?"

Kai was so excited he was getting Luca involved in an actual conversation he didn't care if it was about polar bears.

Kai shrugged, tipping his head from side to side. "Maybe some, but most think of it as a very exotic country far, far away, filled with pretty blond people." He lifted his hand and brushed the back of his fingers over Luca's dark blond hair, making the poor lad look away with his cheeks burning. It was crazy-making in the best way possible. He doubted Luca agreed, but he loved his reactions to him— every single one of them.

They stood up to leave Garbo's and Kai automatically picked up Luca's backpack.

"I can take it," said Luca, pink dusting his cheeks again.

"It's awkward, let me," said Kai gently.

Luca merely nodded, smiling shyly, his Adam's apple bobbing, but he let Kai do it.

They walked for a while, talking about cultural differences. Kai mentioned some other fun ideas Americans had about the land in the north.

"What about the Swedish bikini team, you ever heard of that?"

Luca snorted out a laugh, shaking his head.

"My Dad used to tell me about these TV beer ads that ran in the nineties with half-naked women which they claimed to be part of the Swedish bikini team."

Luca threw his head back and laughed a heartfelt laugh that echoed around them. Kai grinned, watching with intense interest, knowing instinctively it was probably a rare thing for anyone to see Luca do.

They settled at a bar a few blocks away from where they'd first met. It was a small Irish pub with indoor and outdoor seating. They opted to sit outside since the evening was still nice and they had jackets to wear if it cooled down. Kai couldn't stop feeling amazed at how easy it was to get to know Luca, since his initial impression had been that he was always alone and slightly unapproachable.

They sat quietly observing each other and the people around them. It wasn't the awkward kind of silence but rather the good kind. Kai had expected a struggle and many stubborn tries to get close to the man. Yet here they were, hanging out. Kai was starting to suspect people simply didn't accept Luca for who he was. Considering how unaware he was of his effect on people, Kai thought it might be Luca not knowing himself that well, either.

How can he not see how many heads he's turning? Even now, when he's sitting quietly. He doesn't seem to notice the appreciative looks he's getting.

Tipping his head to the side, Kai kept watching Luca. He'd gotten mixed signals from him from get-go and was a little unsure what to make of it. At one moment he was touching freely but, Kai would admit it was mostly when he was preoccupied with something else and didn't seem to be aware of what he was doing, but still it happened, but as soon as he caught himself, he pulled back. Kai wasn't completely sure he knew he was doing it. When Luca relaxed, his subconscious did what he really wanted to do, and when his conscious caught on, he seemed awkward or uncomfortable. Kai decided to let it go for now and listen to his brother Kai's advice for once and be patient. Pushing too much or too hard would only scare him off. Time would reveal what was what.

No matter if he was gay or not, Kai enjoyed his company and wanted to spend more time with him. However, deep in his heart, he already knew he wanted more. Kai was very attracted to Luca and had been from the start. Getting to know him hadn't weakened that feeling, not even a little. He was infatuated with this shy boy from Sweden.

He might be a little disappointed if he wasn't gay. Okay, a lot disappointed but, at the end of the day, he was a great man. And, something told Kai his gut instinct was right. Luca was as much into him as Kai was into Luca. At that exact moment, Luca was watching something which had given him a rueful, almost loving expression on his face. Kai turned slightly to see what had caught his lovely company's attention. Two men, a little older than them, sat at a table farther down, holding hands.

Kai grinned, turning back without Luca noticing and let out a breath he didn't know he'd been holding. Yeah, he was fairly sure he was right. At that moment, Luca looked more beautiful and innocent than Kai had ever seen him. Even though he'd promised himself to take it slow, to not scare Luca away, he couldn't resist reaching out and slipping his hand on top of Luca's.

"You Okay?" Kai asked him with a soft smile, brushing his thumb over the smooth skin on Luca's hand.

Luca nodded slowly, but didn't speak at first, instead he watched as his finger as it moved over the back of his hand. He was fascinated by how a small touch like that could seemed to make Luca's go speechless. It was a good sign, a very good sign and Kai couldn't help but feel a little smug about the fact.

"Yes," he finally whispered, clearing his throat a few times, still not meeting his gaze more than a few seconds a time. "I...we..." their eyes met and time stopped, his thumb was still rubbing over the back of Luca's hand and that moment everything was perfect.

Luca didn't try to speak again instead they sat there looking at each other neither of them able to look away, lost in the sensation of their hands touching.

"You lovebirds ready to order?" The waitress gave them one of those silly cute smiles, like she'd witnessed something unusual. Kai could have screamed at her indiscretion as Luca snatched his hand back, looking away, obviously uncomfortable and probably trying desperately to find a way to escape the situation.

"Two beers from the tap, Carlsberg is fine." Kai gave her a quick smile but all of his attention was really on Luca.

Reaching out but not touching, Kai put his hand next to Luca's arm. "Hey. It's okay. She doesn't know anything; it was a silly remark. It meant nothing. Don't let it ruin our night; you're having fun, aren't you?" Kai put on a brave smile, hoping inwardly he'd be able to get Luca to forget about the waitress' comment and not shut down. *Please, please, pretty Luca, look at me. I won't hurt you, I promise!*

LUCA STARTED TO raise his head enough to see Kai's hand lying next to his arm on the table. He was mortified. What if someone who knew him had seen that? What would they have thought? What would his parents have to say if they knew? He had to stop whatever foolishness was going on before it ruined him.

"I'm sorry... I...I didn't expect that. I'm not homophobic..." Luca lowered his voice, looking around. "Are you... I mean, do you like... Oh, this is not coming out right." Luca brushed a nervous hand over his hair, avoiding looking at Kai and feeling unnerved by the entire situation.

"Luca, breathe. You can ask me anything you want and it's all right. I'll always tell you the truth."

Once again, the mere touch of Kai's hand on Luca's own calmed him. Wasn't that the funniest thing you ever heard? His heart raced like a running horse when they touched but inside he felt...he felt peaceful. It was such an unfamiliar feeling; Luca didn't quite know what to make of it.

"They're strangers and nothing they say matters, okay. To answer your question..." Kai paused for a second and Luca kept looking into his eyes as he waited like it was the most natural thing to do.

"Yes, I'm gay and very open about it, I don't hide it. It's nothing I make a big deal out of, love is love." Kai was silent for a moment, pondering if he was going to tell Luca about watching him and if that would freak him out. Seeing Luca's face after his admission made the decision easy, it was better to tell him now, rather than later. "I'm not expecting anything from you, Luca, but friendship. I'm not going to lie and say that I don't find you extremely attractive but I'd never assume anything. I've actually watched you from a distance for a while, waiting for a chance to talk to you." Kai admitted this with a soft smile while Luca felt like he must look like a baby bird with his mouth hanging open.

"I'm not a creep. I promise!" Kai chuckled, putting his hands up in mock surrender.

Luca felt stunned, moved his lips as if to speak but had to try twice before any sound came out. "You have...? Me? Are you sure? Why? I mean..." Luca waved a hand in the air.

"I'm just me, odd and boring…and, let's face it, a bit of a klutz." He cringed at the thought of his multiple incidents from even that very day and instantly tried to remember what other embarrassing things he'd done for the past few weeks. What had Kai seen when he'd watched him? "Oh, God. I must have looked so stupid!" He slapped a hand over his mouth, squeezing his eyes closed as he uttered the words. He hadn't meant to say that out loud. This entire day had been a long road of bumps and falls. Except, one of those bumps and falls had let him meet Kai.

The past few hours with him had been the most fun he'd had in what seemed like forever. Maybe it was forever, because the way Kai made him feel could only be described with one word—alive. Usually, he couldn't carry a conversation for too long, it always felt forced. With Kai he had no problem talking about what he liked and didn't. It was as if he could be himself around him. *I don't understand how that is? I don't even know him, and still, I don't want this night to end.*

Kai fell silent when the waitress reappeared to put their beers down and waited for her leave before he speaking again. "Why do you do that?" Kai frowned.

"Do what?" He raised his eyebrows. "I don't understand."

"Put yourself down like you do. You are different, yes, an original, Luca, but that's not a bad thing. It was one of the first things that made me see you. I could watch you for hours…" Kai stopped, "You're fascinating." Kai smiled again. "Even more so now than before we officially met."

"I don't see why anyone would watch me." Luca couldn't help squirming in his seat, especially since he was looking at him with those amazing brown eyes. He didn't even know if he liked the fact Kai had watched him without his knowing. Only God knows what kind of embarrassing things he'd done. *Oh, stop it! You know you love the fact that this stud has watched you and liked what he's seen. Stud?* Luca stilled. *Now, where the hell had that come from?*

"You honestly want to know why I watched you?"

Luca didn't say a word, he simply nodded. He didn't dare say anything else.

"First time I saw you, it was in the library here downtown. You were eating a sandwich, I think, and typing away on your laptop. I remember seeing you and stopping because there was this girl who was desperately trying to get your attention. When she was talking to you, you must have helped her but otherwise you didn't see her, or her attempt to get your attention.

"To be honest, I thought you were the best-looking guy I'd ever laid eyes on. But what did it, what made me look for you and on occasion observe you, was when I was about to leave, you looked up. I know you weren't looking directly at me but I saw your eyes and your face fully for the first time. You took my breath away. After that, I saw you from time to time and I wanted to find an opportunity to talk to you, but every time I tried you'd be hurrying away, avoiding anyone who made contact with you. So, I decided to wait…wait for the perfect time."

He could feel his eyes grow huge as he looked at Kai in stunned silence.

* * * *

KAI WATCHED LUCA'S tram leave the stop, following it as it went down the main street called Avenyn. No longer able to see him or the tram, Kai started his walk toward the student apartment he was living in and smiled to himself as he thought of Luca and their evening together. He was painfully shy, but Kai could tell he'd been happy to be there and enjoyed his company, as much as he'd enjoyed Luca's. He was hesitant to show physical affection but Kai had seen the lust and interest light up in his eyes when they'd touched.

Of course, it didn't have to mean a thing but in his mind he'd already decided it did. It had to. Why else would he have reacted the way he did? Those simple touches had made Kai's body react instantly and he'd been happy they'd been sitting with a table to cover up the bulge in his pants. The sudden increase in his pulse wasn't anything anyone could easily pick up on, thank God.

As they said goodbye at the tram stop, he'd wanted so badly to lean in and kissed Luca. He imagined they'd be very soft, but he'd held back, knowing it was most definitely too much, too soon. Instead, he'd brushed his thumb over Luca's cheek as he'd cupped his face, telling him he'd see him soon.

Luca had, as per usual, blushed bright red and taken a step back, looking around, not comfortable with the public affection. It had saddened Kai a little but he shrugged it off as one of those awkward moments when you realize where you are and people are watching.

He crossed the street to cut through the park. The shyness Luca showed was so unfamiliar to Kai; he'd never been a shy person growing up in his loving, open family. They gave him a hard time in a good way, pushing him to be the best he could be, and he'd learned to grow a thick skin.

His father was a remarkable man who'd encouraged his children to see the world, try out other professions besides ranching. There was no force or expectation for any of his children to take over the ranch, but Kai wanted to.

Kit was only a year older than Kai and they were as close as brothers could be. They'd shared most things, including a room—friends, taste in music, more or less everything. Kit was the one he missed the most, and they talked almost every day on the phone. Kit had been the first person Kai had come out to, too. He could still remember how nervous he'd been and afraid Kit would push him away. Yet, Kit had smiled and shrugged a little.

"I know, but if you think that will change anything, you're dumber than I thought." He'd bumped Kai's shoulder in a playful gesture to show him that, as always, he was pulling his chain.

"How did you know?" Kai had asked, because he sure as hell wasn't prissy. Even though they were tight, how could Kit have figured it out, and without telling Kai about it?

"You think I don't see where your eyes are drawn. Besides, you hate sports but go to every damn football practice and game, and I know it's not to show me any support, but to watch Mark and hopefully see him shove his ass in the air."

"You're an ass," Kai had said, and they'd laughed that Kit had been right in his assessment. Kai *did* do that. Mark was gorgeous, with a very muscular and lean body that was to die for. At least, at fifteen, that's what he'd thought. He had nothing else to compare to. So, he spent his sophomore year watching Mark's ass in the air, ignoring the rest of the game. As soon as Mark graduated high school, Kai had stopped going to the games.

After telling Kit that night in front of the TV, it had taken him another six months or so to tell his parents, and Margaret, his sister, the truth about who he was. Kai had felt guilty for not sharing such a big part of himself with them but he was so nervous and scared, even if Kit had told him it would be okay. He was a teenager and that's what teenagers worried about, stupid shit, right?

This was Texas, after all, and his father was in a very old-fashioned business, and not very accepting of anything out of the norm. But the day had come when he hadn't been able or willing to hide who he was anymore. With Kit's presence and support, he'd blurted it out in mid conversation.

"I'm gay!"

Everyone had gone quiet, looking at him like he was nuts, before they actually started to laugh.

"I'm glad you all find this so very amusing." He'd been hurt by their reaction until his dad waved him over with the spatula he'd been holding to work the burgers on the grill. He'd walked over to him, a little annoyed but still interested in hearing what he thought. His dad had put his arm around him, handing him the spatula, telling him to flip the burgers and listen to him carefully.

"Is this why you've been distant the past few months and practically wearing the front lawn down for the past hour?"

Kai had only nodded, studiously flipping burgers and putting some cheese on them as he stood there with a slight pout while his dad hugged his shoulder.

"Well, I'm glad you finally told me…us…but you should have told me sooner, Kai." He'd turned Kai toward him, holding his shoulders and giving him one of those "don't argue with me" looks. "This doesn't change a damn thing, you know that, right? You're still my boy, yes."

It had felt like a heavy load lifted off his shoulders as his dad pulled him in for a hug. Kai's mother had come over, too, cupping his face as she told him how much she loved him. If he thought he was off the hook in giving her grandchildren, he was sorely mistaken. That had set off another round of laughter and that had been that.

Over time, Kai had many conversations with his dad about the ranch and maybe it would be better if Kai chose to do something else.

His dad said each time, "You choose your life, Kai. If you want to do something else, I'll never stop you from reaching your dreams. If working this ranch with me is what your heart desires, then I'd be proud to have you working here beside me. When the day comes for me to retire, this will all be yours. And if someone happens not to like that, then I'll happily show them the door."

With the love and support of his family, Kai had grown up to become a confident, self-assured person. Being gay and living in Texas wasn't always easy, but he'd never once felt ashamed of himself or the urge to hide who he was. Kit had stood up for him numerous times at different events when they'd been out together. His dad had blown up a storm every time one of the workers used the word queer or fagot. He'd said anyone who didn't feel like working there could leave on the spot. Two of the ten workers had left and his only reply had been, "Good riddance!"

He dug through his pants pockets for his keys and stepped into his small apartment. He wondered if Luca had the same support from his family. He couldn't imagine how anyone could do without it. In his world, he could be who he was, as much as he was, because of his family. Sure, there had been times, and still were, when the bigotry got to Kai, and he wanted to tell people to fuck off. He never once doubted himself or felt that he should be ashamed for being gay. His family had made sure of that. He really missed being able to talk to them face-to-face. He picked up his phone, knowing it was mid-afternoon in Texas, and phoned his dad.

"You're up late, son," his father said as he answered his phone on the first ring. Kai chuckled at the speed his father picked up the call, as if he'd been waiting for him to ring.

"It's only ten-thirty. But, yeah, I've been out with a friend. Walking home, I thought of you and mom, all of you actually, and how lucky I am to have you." Kai could imagine the look in his father's eyes, his eyebrow rising in a questioning look. Kai was not the one in the family who freely gave declarations of love out of nowhere.

"Is that so, what brought this all on, Kai?" His father actually sounded worried for a moment and he heard the sound of the truck door slamming shut.

"How do you do that, Dad?" Kai dropped down on his couch, getting comfortable.

"Do what, Son, get in my truck and turn on the AC?" He laughed softly, knowing perfectly well what Kai meant.

"I met someone, Pops. It was only today that we talked for the first time after I've been watching him for weeks like a damn stalker. And I don't know what it is but…it's different."

His dad cleared his throat a little before speaking. Kai knew his dad didn't love these kind of heart-to-heart talks, not because Kai talked about other men. But because he said the lovey-dovey stuff went way beyond his comprehension. He always said, he loved his wife; that was all he knew.

"And this scares you." It was more a statement than a question so Kai didn't reply. "I told you this before, but I'll say it again, my gut and my heart knew your mother was it before my head had sorted everything out. Go spend some time with this boy and see where it takes you."

"Dad, he's hardly a boy and neither am I, but, yeah, you're right. I am scared." He put the phone between his ear and shoulder as he started to pull his boots off. "He's not out of the closet, Dad, and, what if I'm wrong? I think he's in denial even to himself. Maybe I'm setting myself up to get hurt. I don't know what to do, Pops."

"First of all, Kai, you've got to decide if you're going to let fear run your life. You decide what's to be your life, not me, not Mom or working this ranch. You!" This was so his dad—the "action man." He was such a strong believer in "you alone decided your fate" and he told Kai so every chance he got, without ever putting any guilt or pressure on him. He said it matter-of-fact.

"Maybe what he needs right now is a friend, and maybe that's all it will ever be. But, if you're right and he isn't out yet, maybe he needs someone like you to confide in. Don't be selfish and let your own needs run amok. Give him your friendship and be gentle."

"You're right, Pops. Like always. I think I'm more involved than I thought I would be at this point." Hearing his dad turn off the engine and get out of the truck, signaled to Kai his dad had to go. Maybe it was for the best, he had some thinking to do.

"Oh, please, would you tell that to Ma the next time you talk to her? And, Kai, my son, be honest with him without shoving it down his throat. Let him know what your intentions are from the very beginning. It will allow him to make his own decisions and figure himself out. You're a good person, Kai. You know how to be a good friend." His dad slammed the truck door shut; he had to go.

"Okay, Dad. I'll try to chill. Thanks for talking to me. I love you. Tell Ma I love her, too, and I'll talk to you soon."

"No need to thank me, Son. I'm always here for you. Love you, too."

The line went dead.

Kai stripped the rest of his clothes off as he walked into the bathroom to brush his teeth quickly. He turned down the covers and slipped between the cool sheets, thinking about Luca and his phone call with his dad. How cool it actually was that he could call his dad and share something like this with him. As sleep caught him, he decided the next day he'd try to find out where Luca lived. Maybe drop by to say hi, making it harder for the man to turn him down.

CONFRONTATIONS

LUCA WOKE UP the next morning with an unusual feeling of excitement rushing through him. It wasn't like anything he'd ever felt before. If he was to describe it, he'd say he felt nauseated but in a good way, in a *very* good way. It sounded so silly but it was the best description of what was going on inside him.

The first thought popping into his head was the night before and, well, Kai. He couldn't believe the way they'd met and something good had come out of that train wreck. What a day it had been before, during, and after Kai. It still made his cheeks grow hot thinking about how much of a klutz he'd been. God, it had been so embarrassing. How the hell he managed to be twenty and still alive was beyond him. But because of the awkward coffee moment, or in spite of it, Kai had turned out to be this great person. It had been as if they'd known each other forever.

At least it had been for him, still was. Luca had never had a friend of his own or who made him feel the way he did with Kai. Someone he could say anything to, even the silly things, and not feel like a fool. Kai had, from the moment they met, this way of looking at him, as if what he said mattered. It made him forget about his own shyness, and share his inner hopes and dreams, the ones he never shared with anyone. That felt good.

Kai was a complete stranger and yet he didn't hesitate to open up. Luca should have been cautious and wary like he normally was around people, strangers or not. Instead, he'd felt Kai understood him better than anyone in his current life.

Normally he was the outsider, the oddball, the lad no one could relate to—yesterday he hadn't felt like that once. He'd had fun and he'd talked more to Kai in a few hours than he done to anyone in his teenage life.

Maybe it was because Kai was gay? Maybe it was as they said, that gay men were more sensitive to things? He shook his head in dismay, that wasn't it, but there was something about Kai that was more than just the fact that he was kind. Luca couldn't put his finger on what it was but there was something.

The crisp sheets and pillowcases, which were changed every other day by the maid to stay that way, rustled under his head. No, that was a dumb assumption about Kai. Luckily for him, no one could hear his thoughts.

Still, the questions kept echoing in his head.

But how does a complete stranger know you better than those who see you every day? Why aren't I running like my butt's on fire? He admitted to following and watching me. Why aren't I creeped out by that...? Maybe I am, but haven't realized it yet. Because really, that would be the most honest reaction, wouldn't it? He wasn't creeped out he was excited!

Didn't he say he found me attractive...what the hell do I do with that? Does that mean he wants to have sex with me? The fact that he's gay...should be awkward, shouldn't it?

He pondered that for a minute, a little worried about what it meant, what it said about hi because...*it doesn't make it awkward, it's comforting.* Flipping his eyes open, no he wasn't going there, but his mind had already taken the road down to the dark pit of his subconscious where he hid things...things no one knew about him. Things he didn't even admit to himself. But with Kai so fresh in his mind it was like opening Pandora's box and something had spilled out, something that wasn't able to go back inside.

Luca's body went rigid at the thought. Well, something did, at least. He tried to ignore the growing erection going on inside his shorts. *Just stop overthinking everything. Just chill the fuck out!*

It wasn't abnormal to have a morning erection, all men had them, but someone was sure perking up now. At least with girls, he knew to insert stiffy A in slot A, even if he technically hadn't done the particular deed or anything similar with a girl. He couldn't help wondering what men did, but the thought about the possibilities of what that was had him breathing harder. Did they rub one off on each other or only jack each other off? Blow jobs? It had to be, because there was no way in hell there was any truth to the rumor of inserting stiffy A in slot B. No way that was true; it had to be impossible, right?

But the way his heart beat in his chest and the images started to flash through his mind, the idea of that wasn't as unappealing as he wanted it to be. Actually it wasn't unappealing at all.

Staring blankly up at his bedroom ceiling. What the hell did he know about sex anyway, and especially gay sex? And why was he even worrying about not knowing enough about either?

It had to be because of Kai and how open he was about all aspects of himself. It was refreshing and it made Luca look at the kind of person he wished he was. To be honest, it was such a pain in the bum, being shy, afraid to state your opinion, worrying about what was socially acceptable or not. It was like living in two worlds, his parents' world and the real world where everyone else lived.

But talking to Kai had been easy, he'd told him about his home in Texas and why he'd chosen to come to Sweden. Why on earth would you leave the U.S.A. to come here? That was insane. Luca would love the chance to get away from this place and go somewhere no one knew him. Was that why Kai left his home? It hadn't sounded like it, considering the way he'd spoken about his family and home.

Luca grinned to himself, playing with the corner of the sheet covering him, as he thought about the sound of Kai's voice. Even when he tried speaking Swedish, he had a great accent. And when he spoke in English, oh wow, how could you not love the twang. It was, for lack of a better word, very sexy; he could see why girls, or guys for that matter, went all silly around the American boy.

Kai had told him about Texas and their family ranch, how it had been theirs for generations. Exactly like him, Kai was following in his father's footsteps but, unlike Kai, Luca had no choice.

Listening to Kai talk about the acres and acres of land, being on horseback for days, riding and herding cattle, Luca had been jealous. He'd been able to picture himself right there with Kai, working the cattle. That was what he wanted to do. It explained the whole cowboy boots and jeans with the big buckle. If it had been any other person, they would have looked like a damn fool walking around the city of Gothenburg, dressed like someone out of a Western. But not Kai. It actually suited him and made him look all exotic and hot. It was slightly unnerving how awestruck he felt from meeting Kai. You'd think he was people deprived by the way he was acting. Maybe he was?

But it's normal for one man to appreciate the good looks of another. That's normal human behavior. I mean, I'm a guy and he's a guy, I have no interest in males that way, so... I'd better keep this to myself, no point in letting anyone know, truth or not. It's all in my head, no one needs to know. No one needs to know. But he knew.

He rubbed a hand over the sheets nervously. He liked girls, they were...pretty and...things. No doubt about it, he was not...gay. To prove himself right, he tried to think of a girl he liked. Jessica! He liked her a lot actually, she was sweet and they always had fun together. Especially at all those boring dinners they were constantly forced to attend.

They'd usually go off somewhere quiet and talk about random things. Try to have some real fun by playing a game or watching a movie. There, he liked girls. Jessica was great and she was really, really pretty, too. He instantly felt a lot better and could relax back down against the soft pillows.

Yesterday had been one of the best days Luca had had in a long time and he didn't want anything, not even himself, to ruin that. They'd even made plans to see a concert together, there were usually plenty of them going on during the summer. In Varberg, a smaller town right on the coast, south of Gothenburg, they had a lot of outdoor concerts during spring and summer. He was determined to look up a few so, next time, he and Kai would have a few options for them to choose from.

Kai had bounced in his seat with excitement, when Luca suggested they could try to hit the Metal town festival—that came around every year in June—together. A cowboy who preferred metal to country music, that had to be scarce. The thought of going to those concerts with Kai had him so animated, he forgot all about what his parents would think, and the fight he'd have trying to get them to let him have fun for once—the sort that didn't entail his nose stuck in a medicine book. No one was more relieved than Luca when his father's plan for him to work at the University hospital all summer had backfired because Luca had only been a first-year med student.

He'd felt brave when teasing Kai about being a cowboy and not liking country music. The best thing had been when Kai had played along, teasing him back. As his laugh rang out, Luca thought it was one of the most beautiful, real sounds he'd ever heard. Kai had playfully nudged Luca's leg under the table, making his thigh tingle from the simple touch, giving him a mischievous grin, making him even more intriguing.

The most intense moment had been what had followed. "It's not that I mind it, it's more a preference, and I mind it even less if I'm in the mood for a two-step with a pretty partner." He'd winked. What had caused Luca to shift in his seat was when he'd asked what type of dance that was. For what seemed like a very long moment, Kai was quiet, looking at him so strangely he was positive he'd made a fool of himself for not knowing. Then Kai had let his beer go and slid his hand across the table to let his fingers rest on top of his.

"I'll take you dancing and show you some time."

Mesmerized by the intense look in Kai's eyes, Luca's heart beat so hard he could hear the drumming in his ears. His lips had parted to let more air into his lungs and to stop the spinning going on inside his head. But he'd still felt lightheaded.

It had been the second time Kai had physically touched him in a matter of minutes, and Luca knew it should have made him uncomfortable but it didn't. Instead, it excited him and he'd wanted more of it. That had scared him to death. It wasn't until he looked down at their joined hands that Luca realized what Kai meant by his words.

He still wondered if he might have overreacted by pulling his hand away or if Kai had meant it as he'd interpreted it. That he'd wanted to take him on a date. Luca hadn't been able then, or now, to figure out what the suggestion meant, so he'd pulled his hand back and looked away, changing the subject. It had just been easier.

Glancing at his alarm clock, he realized he had at least another twenty minutes before his mother would be knocking on his door. Not even weekends were fully his to enjoy. But he had twenty minutes, and he wasn't going to let them, or his excitement, to go to waste. He let out a deep, contented sigh. Oh, how he wished he could have another day like yesterday. He'd felt invincible, almost free.

Letting his eyelids fall shut, he let his mind wander, as if it was easy to let himself go and study Kai without anyone knowing. Only thoughts, nothing special about that. Everyone did it. Kai's smiling face appeared before him, those deep golden brown eyes smiling at him, looking at him as though he mattered. Luca had never met anyone with such expressive eyes or who looked at him the way Kai had.

"Oh God, Luca." He dramatically slid down the pillows and landed on the mattress with a thud. "What the hell are you doing? If anyone heard you, they'd commit you for a psych evaluation."

Burying his face in his hands, he breathed deeply for a few seconds. He should stop this daydreaming about Kai and get on with his day. He would, he promised himself. He'd only allow himself one moment longer. What harm could one tiny daydream do? None.

He lay there, pushing the real world and the warning signals from his nagging conscience aside, and let himself fantasize about Kai. Before he knew it, his dick was poking the sheets. If he rolled his hips, he could almost feel the soft rasp from his underwear.

Without thinking further, Luca slipped his hand inside his boxers, curling his fingers around his prick, gasping the second he touched warm flesh. Touching himself had never felt so right.

Giving himself a few good pumps, he stroked his cock in long, even strokes, letting the red, swollen tip push through his foreskin. Oh, God, it felt so intense! Usually, when he jacked off, he didn't think about anything or anyone special. It was something he did to relieve tension. Now, with Kai's face before him, it was magnified by a hundred, at least.

He opened his eyes to watch a couple of drops of precum pool at the tip and slowly roll down his shaft. He licked his lips, spellbound by it. Fuck, it was hot, being this turned on, feeling so much. The slick made the tip of his prick glisten. Using his thumb to smear the silky fluid over the head, he massaged his knob. His back arched off the bed, and he moaned loudly into the otherwise silent room, if you didn't count his heavy breathing.

"Oh, fuck." He exhaled a loud groan, imagining the touch being Kai's hand instead of his own. The thought alone made Luca cry out and he had to breathe through his nose as he bit his lip hard to keep himself from coming on the spot.

But, he couldn't hold off any longer. His hand moved over his cock, and he met each movement with a snap of his hips, pushing through the tight tunnel of his hand. It didn't take long before his chest was heaving, and he was trying to catch his breath.

He kept picturing Kai's smiling face in front of him, the muscle-bound body hiding underneath all those clothes and remembering the sweet twang-y voice, as smooth as honey. Heating up, he kicked off the sheet, letting it pool by his feet, pushing his boxers down to his knees in a single move. He gasped as the cool air hit his sensitive skin, making everything feel more acute.

"Oh, my God! I'm...fuck...oh...umph..." His hand was almost flying, legs moving restlessly over the mattress, with no way of stopping it, even if he'd wanted to. His orgasm rolled through, coming so hard he lost the ability to breathe. Heat spread through him like fire as his dick twitched in his hand, spurting cum all over his fingers and stomach, until his body was lax and he sank back heavily into the mattress. His body felt boneless, the idea of moving to clean up fleeting. He felt amazing, though.

"Damn...that...wow..." Few things had ever made him feel this good. Why had he never tried this before? Because Kai hadn't been in his life before now...

Thinking is overrated, Luca. Why do you always have to ruin everything with overthinking? He could easily lie there, take a nap, and when he woke up, do it all over again. However, the chance of him getting to do that was slim to none, knowing his mother. He knew she'd never let that fly, even if he managed to turn his overactive mind off. If he wasn't up by nine, even on weekends, she'd come and wake him up. It was only fifteen minutes short of nine now.

He looked down at his hand, covered with his own seed. He couldn't believe that thinking about Kai had made him come harder than he'd ever done before. His body shivered involuntarily at the thought, it had been so good yet so bad, all at the same time.

A soft heat tingled at his neck and cheeks and he knew what that meant. What had he done? It wasn't so much the deed itself—it wasn't the first time he'd jerked off—but who he'd been thinking of while doing it.

Shame filled him and, in a panic, he turned around, grabbing a few tissues from the nightstand before starting to clean himself off while trying to pull his boxers back up. He barely had time to wipe himself off when there was a knock on the door and his mother walked in.

"Luca, you're up. I know it is not quite nine but your father and I are going out for the day."

He pulled his knees up and rested his arms on them to cover his chest, causing his mother to give him a confused look.

"Are you all right? You're not getting ill, are you?" She reached out and put the back of her hand on his forehead to see if he felt hot. He didn't want her coming near him, he was sure he reeked of sex and was positive if she came any closer, she'd smell cum on him. In an attempt to divert her and get her to step away, Luca turned his head away and rolled his eyes at her. His pulse was still beating hard from the feeling of getting caught or, rather, her finding out what he'd done mere minutes before.

"No, Mother, come on, I just woke up, nothing else. I'm not a kid, stop treating me like one." He was a little snappier than he meant to be but, what the hell? Why knock if you aren't going to wait for an answer? She always did that, and it was getting really annoying. Wow! Being interrupted mid orgasmic bliss was apparently not a good thing if he let his mother's usual behavior affect him so. *Hmm... Interesting.*

"Well, aren't we in a bad mood this morning?" She chuckled and picked up the pants and shirt he'd thrown in a pile on the floor the evening before and put them on his chair. "Maybe you should take a day off from the books and go out and enjoy yourself with a movie or something, honey."

He was about to protest about her touching his things when her words finally hit him. He snorted, thinking she was being sarcastic.

"Huh? I'm allowed to have fun? I thought I was destined to study day and night for the next seven years. *'Luca, school is a serious matter; this is your future we're talking about. There's no time for slacking off.'*" He mimicked his dad's voice while waving his hand around like he usually did when he was giving "the talk."

She laughed a little, but looked slightly bothered. At least his mother had some sort of humor, even if she shared all his father's beliefs on what was good behavior and doing what was expected. Looking at the door, probably to make sure his father wasn't within earshot, she leaned in, taking his face in her hand.

"Your father does tend to get a little carried away at times, but like I said, we're going out for the day. And you're right, my little Luca you are no more. So, do as you please with your day." She kissed him on the cheek, giving him a gentle smile before leaving, closing the door behind her.

He watched the closed door for a long time, shaking his head at his mother. At moments like this, she was such a great mum, warm, caring, and even-humored, but the minute she was in the same room with one of those other society wives, it was like the devil had taken possession of her body.

Luca looked down at himself and sighed as he saw the messy sheets. Doing what he'd done to cover himself up had helped clean him up but the sheets were a horrible mess.

Getting up, he pulled them from his bed. He'd put them in the washer before getting the coffee going and taking a shower. By the time he was done with breakfast, he could let the sheets dry on the line in the sun outside. He loved the spring wind scent of clean sheets.

Looking out his bedroom window while stripping the bed, he watched his parents leave. Maybe, if he put a sweatshirt on, he could sit outside in the sun having breakfast on the deck. He could start reading the book he'd wanted to read for a while now but never seemed to have the time for. He thought of what his mum had suggested about taking a day off and, hell, maybe she was right. He did deserve a day off and the weather was great. Besides, who was he to defy his mum, and it wasn't like his dad would ever find out. Luca was doing way too well in school; no one would notice if he slacked off for one day.

Grinning like a fool, he picked up his phone from the nightstand and scrolled until he found Kai's number, putting it into an empty text message. He wanted to text him to say "thank you," because he'd had a great time, and it was the polite thing to do, right? What happened this morning, that had been wrong but no one would ever know. He swallowed hard, tapping his phone rather nervously and began to type.

Hi Kai, thank you for a great time yesterday...

He stopped what he was doing, realizing how corny it sounded and deleted the message to start afresh. *Less corny, Luca, think more cool. Stop being such a child and act natural!* He sat there looking at the blank screen—he had no idea what to write.

Holding his phone, he dragged his free hand through his hair, letting out an annoyed curse. That was something he rarely did because, again according to his father, nice boys and girls didn't. Luca's father used to wash his mouth out with soap when he was little to make him stop bad habits like sucking his thumb. Like most kids, he'd rebel or curse. Somewhere along the line, Luca had managed to learn that all these things were wrong, but for him it had been normal. He'd never really talked to anyone about it. Who would listen? Returning his attention to the phone in his hand, Luca tried to think rationally.

How hard can it be to write one, casual text? I mean, really?

After another moment, he gave up and put the phone back down, too annoyed with himself to make anything of it. Standing up, he collected the sheets in his arms with a jerk. Why would a simple thing like sending someone a text makes him freeze up like that? Why was he making such a big deal out of meeting Kai? He really needed to get his head around this whole thing with him and get over it already. Maybe *not* sending him a text was a good thing, and maybe seeing him again wouldn't be such a good idea, either, considering what he'd done earlier.

All in all, when would he have time for a friend, a real friend, between school and the functions his parents expected him to attend? There was little time left for him to do as he pleased. Luca nodded in agreement with his own thoughts, and stepped out of his bedroom to walk toward the washroom. Yeah, this was a good thing.

Then why did it make him feel so sad and lonely?

Half an hour later, he was seated outside on the deck, with his sunglasses on and his Kindle in his lap, letting the sun warm him. Enjoying the fact he had the whole day to himself without anyone else around. Heaven in a bottle! Picking his Kindle back up, he turned it on. Leisure reading wasn't something he had a lot of time to do these days. The fact he could sit here with a clean conscience and read a book purely because he wanted to and not because he had to, was a luxury.

No matter how nice this was, it couldn't measure up to yesterday, but Luca had a feeling few things would for some time. Letting out a deep sigh, he returned his attention to his Kindle. He decided to give this new book he'd read about, it was an erotic LBGT book but it was supposed to be good and he didn't care.

He realized that not only was it was an erotic novel, but it was about four men living together. He felt so bold, reading something so different, so taboo. Getting comfortable, he started to read.

He'd gotten into the book and to a good steamy part when he was interrupted by someone coming up the driveway. He let out a deep sigh at the interruption; he was too intrigued by the four different men and wanted to get lost in them. Luca hoped whoever it was would be quick, and he'd soon be left to relax and read.

Closing the leather folder of his Kindle, he looked up, expecting a neighbor or some other acquaintance of his parents. Instead, the person standing there was someone who not only made his heart skip a beat but made his Kindle slip into his lap without another thought—Kai.

He'd stopped as he saw Luca and tilted his hat back, giving him a big smile as he took a few steps closer.

"Morning, Luca. I'm happy I found you." He smiled, took off his baseball cap and flipped it over in his hand, playing with it. "I hope you don't mind me looking you up?"

Kai gave him one of the radiant smiles that made his entire face light up. Why would he mind? It was Kai, here, at his house! Luca stood up and walked down the steps, stopping on the last one, a little unsure of what to do next. Luca couldn't believe he was here, in front of his house, smiling at him. His heart ran wild in his chest, making it hard to breathe.

"How...how did you find me?" he managed to say as he mimicked Kai's wide smile.

Kai fiddled with his hat before meeting Luca's eyes again. "I looked you up online and thought I'd come and say hi. I hope you don't mind that I did."

Hell! Was he kidding? Why would Luca mind? He'd been wanting to text Kai since he woke up but hadn't been able to work up the nerve, or figure out what to say. Keeping his cool—or trying to—Luca shifted his weight from one foot to the other, still smiling at Kai as he took the last step down so they were standing face-to-face.

"No, no, I don't mind at all. I'm glad you did." Neither of them said anything for a while. Luca started to get uncomfortable with the silence and the intense gaze Kai was aiming at him.

"You want to come inside?" Luca gestured and pointed behind him to the porch. At least it would get them moving and break the trance of standing there, looking at each other. His face flushed as he thought of what he'd done not too long ago, thinking about the man before him. What if he could tell? Would he be mad? Spinning around on his heel, Luca started up the stairs. "I was about to have something cold to drink if you're interested," he said to fill the silence.

Kai gave him a nod and another bright smile. "I'd like that very much."

He heard Kai move behind him, his steps light for a man as tall as him, but his presence was strong, so strong that

Luca could almost feel the heat from Kai's body as he moved slowly behind him.

Oh God, help me!

"Cool. Come on inside, and we can chat." He felt a little confused and worried. Where the hell was the talkative lad from yesterday? The five-word sentences didn't seem like Kai to him. But what the hell did Luca know? It wasn't like he actually knew him, right?

He opened the porch door fully and his breath caught in his throat as Kai's arm brushed his chest as he passed him. Seconds later, Luca had to rub the spot to make sure he was still whole, that the light touch hadn't burnt a hole right through him. This was so weird. More than weird, it was strange and scary to the point of driving him mad! The pull of Kai's presence was so immediate, all he wanted to do was reach out and let his hands slide down Kai's broad back. Luca took a moment to collect himself while Kai looked around. Feeling slightly better, he used "getting drinks" as an excuse to walk into the kitchen and put some distance between them.

"You have a very nice home. I can't believe how close to water you live. That must be really nice. It takes hours for us to get to the ocean." Kai looked in his direction with a boyish grin on his face. "We have this pond about a mile from the house that we used to go to in the summer as kids to swim, but that's pretty much it. Nothing like you have here, of course. The real deal."

"Yeah, I guess it's okay. You get kind of used to it when you live here all year around. I bet Texas is really nice, too, with all those long stretches of ranches, farms, and land, of course. I love animals. If I could, I'd work with them instead of people. So, what would you like? Coke, beer, or water?"

Kai continued to look around but, after another minute, he leaned against the doorframe leading outside to the porch before pushing away and turning back toward Luca.

"A Coke would be great, thank you. So, why don't you? If working with animals is what you'd like to do, why don't you become a veterinarian?" His voice sounded curious, like he really wanted to know the answer. He stepped into the kitchen, and leaned against the counter, watching Luca as he took two soft drinks from the fridge, handing one to Kai.

"Um...my dad...he's a surgeon." Luca shrugged, feeling a little embarrassed that he couldn't stand up to his own father. "It's okay, though. I don't mind." Well he did, but there wasn't any point in debating it, it wasn't like he had a choice in the matter anyway. Getting self-conscious under Kai's intense gaze, he squirmed a little, lifting his drink to his lips and sipping, to have something to do.

"Oh, maybe he'll change his mind, huh?" Kai said, giving him another radiant smile. Luca saw he wanted to say more but held back. Yeah, that's what he usually did, too, when his dad was in the conversation. There was nothing to say. It was his way or the highway, no middle ground. And no gray areas.

He refused to think of him and his ways at this particular time and pushed his father from his mind. Kai was here, a new friend, and he was going to enjoy it. He didn't have many friends, only Jessica, but they never really hung out unless there was some society gathering they both had to go to. Besides, Jessica wasn't a boy. Kai was the first real male friend he'd had in years. Sure, he talked to people at times but not like they had. Luca tried desperately to find something to say, but it was hard to concentrate when Kai was looking at him the way he did. He wasn't quite sure what the look was—not sad, but upset or worried or something.

"Why are you looking at me like that? Do I have dirt on my face or something?" He tried to joke to ease some of the tension but it only increased as Kai moved closer. Luca was in a trance and, unable to move, he could only watch Kai as he put his drink on the counter and kept coming closer until their bodies almost touched. He stopped with inches to spare.

"How am I looking at you, Luca?" The question might have sounded simple but the way he said it, and how close he was standing—very close—made it difficult for Luca to think.

"Like…like, I don't know. What is it…sad maybe, sorry. I don't get why. There's so many things I don't understand." Frustrated. He was so damn frustrated; everything seemed so complicated. Rubbing the back of his neck nervously, he tried to back up to get some space between them. He wanted to be, to feel normal like everyone else, and maybe be happy for more than a few hours once a year. Looking up and into Kai's eyes, he saw pity. Damn!

"Don't feel sorry for me!" He wouldn't have it. Luca was pathetic, he knew that. But he couldn't take Kai—who yesterday had looked at him like he mattered—looking at him with pity in his eyes. He thought he'd finally met someone who understood. Who understood him.

"But I do feel sorry for you, Luca. It's so obvious how much you struggle to please—I can only assume—your dad." Kai took a step forward, and Luca stepped back.

"That's sad. Because you're trying so desperately to be happy, and I think I know why you aren't. Well, partly anyway." He kept coming closer, and Luca was about to throw a fit if he didn't stop.

"Don't!" He held up a hand, stopping Kai. "What the hell are you talking about?" Luca felt doubtful, pleading with Kai not to see him, but there was no disbelief in the pit of Kai's kind gaze, only understanding and knowledge.

"Have you tried talking to your dad about your hopes and dreams? Maybe he doesn't understand how unhappy you are?"

Luca rolled his eyes, yeah right, that was it. "I'm not unhappy. I have a good life, a great life even… You…you don't know me," he stammered. "You don't know me," he whispered, pushing back farther, his back hitting the wall, trapping him between it and Kai.

"Then what do you call this you're doing? This is not happy, Luca, I know happy. And I do know you better than you think. I've been watching you, remember? I'm just like you."

Luca was grateful Kai wasn't moving closer, but also disappointed. It was the strangest feeling. He had no idea why he was so disappointed. Ridiculous!

"Are you always this nervous around men or is it just me?" Kai's voice had grown darker but his eyes were the same, and there was a smile on his face. Still, the change of voice affected Luca, making his stomach flutter with butterflies. Swallowing repeatedly, he licked his lips to gain time and come up with something smart to say.

Every fiber in his body was on alert by the sudden change in the air. He had to get Kai to leave. This was getting way out of hand. He couldn't do this, whatever *this* was, that hung between them. He was getting excited, his body reacting to Kai in a way that wasn't normal for a boy to react to another boy, and it wasn't him. No! He shook his head, he couldn't. He was doomed if he did.

Yet, the sound of Kai's voice felt like the sweetest caress and his face was really close to his. It was hard to focus on being rational and not reach out to run his hands through Kai's hair or trail the contours of his face with his fingers. The need to do so was growing each second he denied himself. His fingers twitched and it took every ounce of willpower to keep his hands at his sides. *Why was he doing this? Please go away!* Luca felt like a trapped, wild animal, ready to lash out and defend himself. His heart was thundering in his chest and ears, making him almost deaf to any other sound.

"I…" Clearing his throat, he felt like his eyes were darting all over the place. "I'm not nervous!" Was that him screaming? He had no idea what hit him, but instead of keeping his head down, he took a chance and stuck his chin up, meeting Kai's eyes with confidence. He said again—with more conviction, as if he was trying to convince himself more than Kai, "You don't make me nervous. I may be a little particular about my personal space." He pushed at Kai's chest to pass him, making a point of doing so. "I'm not more or less nervous around guys than girls. I'm not into men."

Luca felt proud of himself but his heart was drumming hard in his chest. He'd stood up for himself, taken a stand. Kai hadn't stopped watching him the entire time, his face serious, as if he didn't believe what he was seeing. It was probably the first time Luca hadn't seen a smile in those eyes. They were always glowing and lively, even if the rest of his face was casual.

"Is that why you read gay literature? Because you're not into men?" He pointed at the Kindle, barely visible on the table outside the door.

"Is that why you shiver ever every time I touch you? Yesterday, when you didn't think about it, you reached out and touched me. It wasn't a slap on the back either, Luca." Their eyes locked together, heat flowing between them like an electric current, the tension so alive, you could touch it. Luca wanted to object but, in two quick steps, Kai was right there next to him, his fingers covering his lips.

Oh! Luca gasped. So warm.

"Look at you." Kai's fingers moved gently over his lips and the urge to flick his tongue out to taste the warm and slightly roughened skin was overwhelming. "You're nervous."

"No...no...no..." *Look away, Luca. Tell him to leave. He's trying to ruin you! Tell him to leave! He's lying!* But Kai was still there, touching him, setting his skin on fire, making his body sing.

"Have you ever thought about why you don't ever feel like you fit in or can be yourself? But with me, you've been able to do both, and in a short time, too?"

Luca jerked as if he'd been slapped in the face, taking a couple of steps back.

"Why are you doing this? Leave me alone! And stop snooping around in my stuff! First you stalk me, and now this. What the hell!"

Please! Please! Go away, leave me alone, don't do this, I can't. Please!

Luca couldn't deal with this or take it. *No!* He was feeling the panic roar inside him. *No more.* The panic; so brutal, his vision blurred, making it hard for him to focus on anything.

"Luca?" Kai's voice sounded worried even to him. "I'm sorry, Luca. I picked it up to see what you were reading. You looked so into your book when I came. I meant nothing by it, well nothing menacing, at least."

Luca stared at Kai in disbelief, not saying a word. His body was stiff as Kai came up to stand opposite him but not touching. "I'm trying to help you."

"How...? For your information, I read a lot of different books and if you care to know, that particular book has gotten high reviews for more than the fact that it happens to include a couple of men fucking!" he nearly yelled. He could hear himself and how silly he sounded, but he didn't care. Technically, it was four men fucking—quite a lot—but who was counting, or keeping tabs?

"And, really, I don't have to explain myself to you! I read whatever I goddamn well please!" Luca had no idea when he'd gotten so angry but all of a sudden, he was furious and laid it all out for Kai to see. Meeting Kai's eyes, straightening his shoulders and sticking his chin out, he met his gaze head on and burnt a hole into him, refusing to turn his eyes away. Kai had become serious but instead of looking mad or upset, he was studying him. The look he was getting was more of another round of pity which didn't sit well with Luca at all. Who the hell did he think he was? Damn anyone for feeling sorry for him.

"Look, I'm sorry if I pushed too hard, too fast. Let's talk about this," Kai said, taking a step forward, causing Luca to back off right away, not wanting Kai close to him, least of all, touching him. "I pushed too much, too soon. It wasn't my place. If my assumptions are wrong, then I'm sorry. But, like I said, it's hard to know because you're sending me some mixed signals here, Luca."

Luca shook his head, wrapping his arms around him like a security blanket. "Maybe you should go." Luca pointed at the door with his chin, feeling his heart sink to his knees. He stood his ground, though, refusing to show Kai any of the emotion he was feeling. At least, he hoped he wasn't showing any. He tightened his arms around his body to protect himself from Kai's piercing eyes, looking at his feet.

"Come on, please, Luca. I didn't mean to be so blunt. Please don't shut me out, please. I want to get to know you and be a friend, someone you can talk to. I know how scary this is, but you aren't alone."

Luca's heart ached, it literally ached, hearing the pleading in Kai's voice. He lifted his head to look at him again, wanting nothing more than to forgive, forget, and start over. But he was scared. They didn't know each other and still Kai had been able to step right into his center and get him off balance within minutes of meeting. He couldn't let himself go, there would be nothing to find there but heartache. He'd been fooling himself, thinking he could take a moment for pretend and make-believe. He shook his head and the voice coming out of his throat didn't sound anything like him. It was raw, almost painful.

"No. Just...just go...please." He tightened the grip around himself, turning away and giving Kai his back. From the corner of his eye, he could see Kai taking a few steps back, hesitantly taking his hat from the counter and turning to walk out of Luca's life before he even got the chance to know him. The tightness around Luca's chest made him rub his hand over his heart. Kai stopped in the doorway and turned slightly to look at Luca with sadness showing in his face.

"Luca, please. I'm sorry, okay. I want to help you."

"No one can help me." The words were whispered. "Now leave." Luca looked away. He couldn't bear to see the hurt in Kai's eyes. He was hurt himself, angry, and sad.

"I'm very sorry for upsetting you, Luca. To push you away and make you scared was never my intention. I don't hold it against you for sending me away. I can handle that, but maybe you should ask yourself, how long do you think you'll be able to lie to yourself? I honestly don't understand why you would want to. If you ever change your mind and need anyone to talk to, who knows how it is, you have my number."

Luca didn't say a thing, or look at Kai. Instead, he stood glued to the same spot he'd been standing in for the past ten minutes, listening to Kai as he walked away.

REGRETS

KAI HADN'T GOTTEN far when he suddenly stopped walking. He was merely standing there, in the middle of the street, asking himself how everything had gone so wrong, so fast. He'd barely made it inside the door before he'd managed to put his foot in it and after that everything had turned to shit. All because he had to push. His brother Kit would have rolled his eyes, clucked his tongue, and patted him on the head like a little boy if he'd been there. He could hear him scolding—"you're too pushy"—and pointing out how he always wanted things his way immediately, instead of hearing what other people had to say.

He could kick himself for making Luca so uncomfortable he'd rejected him. He also felt sorry for Luca for having so much trouble with his own sexuality. At least, he thought he did. What else could it be? He'd been getting mixed signals from him since they'd met. Yes, he was jumpy, but he hadn't denied his touch, and the look in his eyes when he'd seen the gay couple had been almost blissful.

It might make him sound arrogant, but he knew blissful when he saw it. It was sort of obvious to Kai that Luca was as attracted to him as Kai was to Luca, but he refused to see it, least of all acknowledge it out loud. It pissed him off no end someone as sweet as Luca was forced to live a lie. To live like that, he had to completely deny himself and believe his own lies.

He'd known from watching over the past few weeks that Luca was the most conservative and private person Kai had ever met. That was saying a lot since he came from the Old

South. But it showed in everything he did, how he dressed, spoke, and carried himself. It wasn't that he was unapproachable, he'd proved that fairly easily, but he became silent and shut down in any sort of social situation as if he didn't know how to be himself.

"Damn it!" Ripping his hat off, he threw it down on the bench next to him as he lowered himself onto it and rested his head in his palms. He rubbed his eyes with the heel of his hands so hard, he could almost feel them protrude from the back of his head.

There were so many things about Luca's behavior that were oddly cute, for lack of a better word, but they were also landmines for something deeper. A well-kept secret Luca didn't seem to want to share with anyone, not even himself.

Luca keeping to himself made a lot more sense now. In the classroom and structured environments, he was more confident because it was all about learned skills and facts. He knew what others expected of him and acted accordingly. Outside, it was about being himself. Without the honesty needed to face up to who he was, he lost all his confidence.

Kit sometimes called Kai naive because he was so used to a family who loved and supported him that he didn't realize not everyone had that. Spending time with Luca one on one had proved he hadn't realized, or fully understood, what Kit had been saying.

He seldom doubted his gut, or who he was—he was comfortable with himself. Luca obviously wasn't. He could hear his brother, even though he wasn't there, telling him to get a grip and stop bulldozing people if he wanted them to stick around.

Groaning to himself, Kai rested his elbows on his knees, his chin in his hands, pondering his options. How could he have been so damn stupid? What had he been out to prove with a man he'd known less than a day? Why had it been so damn important to find out if Luca was gay, that very instant? Well, the answer was easy. He was hooked, already deeply infatuated with Luca. Knowing him or not, the shy, tall Swede had taken up a permanent place on the threshold of his heart.

What was he supposed to do? Maybe he should leave Luca alone, let the poor lad deal with it all on his own, and not put any more pressure on him. And, at the same time, cut his losses before he got in any deeper. Getting involved with someone who was that deep in denial would only cause him heartache in the end.

Kai shook his head; no, he didn't feel comfortable with that. He'd opened Pandora's Box. The least he could do was to be Luca's friend, and maybe help him answer a few of the questions he probably had about himself. He nodded absently, *yeah, that was a good idea.* You could never have too many friends, and they could *be* friends. *No problem.*

Who's lying now, Kai thought, but he pushed the thought away, instantly refusing to listen to the warning bells ringing in the back of his mind.

Luca needed someone to see him and help him feel comfortable in his own skin. Kai needed to find a way to show Luca what it meant to be alive. He needed a good friend. If nothing else, he had to at least see him again to apologize for upsetting him.

Kai grabbed his baseball cap as he stood and walked to the tram station. Once more, he thought about the mixed signals. He knew it was like beating a dead horse, but he was obsessed. He wanted there to be something other than only his feelings involved because if he was wrong and Luca really wasn't interested, then he stood no chance. He refused to accept that as yet.

The air between them had been charged with heat, and the way Luca had looked at him when he first arrived, his eyes growing larger as if he was happily surprised he was there. His lips had parted, only to close and break into a great smile, taking a breath as if he couldn't believe Kai was there and he was trying not to show how happy it made him. That moment alone had made Kai feel like a million bucks, and his nerves had been working him over all morning, had started to calm. He, who seldom got nervous, had it so bad he barely knew what to say. That never ever happened to him. Like never.

Kai really wanted to talk to his brother, but it was almost four in the morning at home. Screw it; Kit wouldn't be too mad if he woke him. He grabbed his phone before speed dialing his brother's number. The phone rang a few times before there was a sleepy voice on the other end.

"Hello…"

"Hey, Kit, it's me…I'm sorry to wake you up." He paused for a second, thinking about what to tell him without sounding like a fool. "Do you have a minute, I think I messed up bad, and I need you to help me fix it." Kai could hear Kit move under the sheets, most likely getting into a more comfortable position.

"Does this have anything to do with that dude Dad said you met?"

"What the hell? Did he call you right after we spoke?" They both knew you didn't keep a secret for long in the Kelly household.

"No, not at all, I was there with him the whole time you talked but since you were having a moment, I kept my mouth shut." The teasing tone of Kit's voice felt good, and Kai chuckled a little. He loved his brother to death, but he was a damn tease. Kit used every chance he got to do it, too. The good thing with Kit, though, was that he could always make you smile and feel better when you were down about something.

"Screw you, Kit!" He laughed, instantly feeling better. "We weren't having a moment... Oh, you're both buttheads! You're as bad as he is, you know?"

"No, I'm worse, but who's keeping track?"

Hearing the wide grin in Kit's voice made Kai shake his head, choosing to take his words as a compliment. Joking around with Kit gave him a familiar feeling, like a warm blanket draping around him. It made him miss home and his family enough to make his heart ache.

"So, are you going to tell me what happened to this man of yours?"

"He's not mine and, considering how well I put my foot in my mouth a while ago, I don't think he'll ever be close to being my anything. It's a mess, Kit."

He told Kit the short version of the day before and how they'd talked for hours without a glitch. It was fun and easy talking about his and Luca's evening, because, overall, it had been a really good night. The hard stuff was telling Kit about this morning. How everything had been perfect from the moment Luca laid eyes on him until Kai questioned his sexuality and kept pushing.

Kit was silent for a long moment after he was done.

"You're making assumptions here, Kai. Maybe he *isn't* into dudes. You're not known to take things slow."

Kai opened his mouth to protest.

"Oh, hush, save the protest. We both know I'm right."

Kai closed his mouth again, narrowing eyes, scolding his brother silently.

"Look, maybe be his friend for now and see what comes. By the sound of it, the two of you hit it off pretty damn good. That could scare anyone who wasn't prepared for it. Especially if you're convinced you're not attracted to the same sex."

Kit stopped for a moment and took a breath before he continued.

"Kai, I've said it before. You're lucky because you have us to support you and love you, no matter what. That's the way it's supposed to be. But, from the sound of it, this dude doesn't have that, so you need to give the poor bastard a break. Maybe that's why you two have met, you know, for you to help him deal with this so he can find himself?"

Stunned by what Kit told him, Kai had to take a second. He was looking at his phone like it had grown a head and was talking back at him.

"Wow…I don't know what to say to that, Kit. I never knew you were so damn deep," Kai said, baffled. "Where the hell did all that come from?"

Kai watched the people getting off the tram, which had shortly before pulled up. He saw them, but they barely registered. "You really think that's it?"

Kit let out a sigh, and Kai could hear him moving around before he answered.

"Honestly, I don't know, but it sounded good, didn't it? No seriously, I don't know, Kai. You want me to have the answer for you as to what this is and how it will end. You know I can't. You have to decide if he is worth the risk, and the effort. I guess, if it was me, I'd ask myself if I'd regret not doing something while I had the chance."

The platform was once again empty, and he'd missed another tram heading downtown, but he was pretty sure he wasn't going back.

"So, how do I fix this? He was really upset when I left and, hell, Kit, I don't really know him."

There was a loud yawn on the other end of the line.

"You do what all men do when they've done wrong, you grovel. Got to sleep, baby bro, love you."

Kai said his goodbyes to Kit and ended the call. He sunk to the bench, thinking hard. Kit was right, there were no guarantees of anything, not even if everything had gone smoothly and this had never happened. So, it was up to him to figure out if it was worth it or not. In a way, he'd already made up his mind some time ago, hadn't he? He wouldn't have gone through all this trouble finding out about Luca, checking him out, going out of his way to meet him, if it meant nothing. He wasn't about to stand up and walk away the second things got a little rough. It wasn't in Kai's nature to do that generally, so why start with this?

"Grovel, huh? Okay, let's do this, Kelly."

He stood up, readying himself to go back to Luca's house. Damn, he really didn't want Luca to push him away. Nor did Kai want to give up on him, Luca had really captured him in a way no one had for a long time.

"Keep it simple, apologize. Stay friends. *No* pushing!" he told himself as a woman on a bike went past, smiling at him. She probably felt sorry for him and thought he needed it because talking to yourself indicated you were going insane. He started to slowly walk back the way he'd come, thinking about what to say. Also, he wondered how to get Luca to open the door in the first place. The thing was, he'd never had to grovel in his entire life. Not really. He realized how damn easy his dating life had been, or was it the men he'd met who had been easy? He had no idea. But he couldn't go back there until he figured this shit out.

It was obvious Luca didn't respond well to being pushed and cornered, so going back there demanding things wouldn't do him any favors.

"Hello there, young man." Kai snapped out of his thoughts, seeing the elderly woman who had stopped next to him.

"Hello there, Ma'am," he said in broken Swedish.

"Oh, you're not from here." She smiled as he shook his head, trying to keep up with what she said. It was harder at the moment because he wasn't in the right mindset to speak to little old ladies in the street, no matter how sweet they seemed. "Are you lost?" she asked, patting his arm. "You look a little worried. I'd be happy to help."

Kai couldn't help smiling, putting his hand on hers.

"You're too kind. I'm not lost, thank you. I feel a little bad because I upset a friend. Now I have to figure out how to make him forgive me."

"Oh, but all friends have disagreements at times. I'm sure if you tell him you're sorry and mean it, then he'll forgive and forget," she replied kindly.

"I'm not too sure about that. But, I'll figure something out, I hope. Thank you, though, for your concern. I really do appreciate it." Kai tried to give her a sincere smile.

She tipped her head to the side. "Is this boy your sweetheart?"

He raised an eyebrow, knowing he probably looked as surprised as he felt.

"I may be old, young man, but I'm not a fool. If you upset your sweetheart, you need to plead, and beg. We all know that. Flowers are good *and* chocolates." She counted off her fingers before stopping and looked up at him. "But do you know what works the best?"

Kai could only shake his head. This little old lady was a firecracker. She was adorable!

"A clean heart and honest words. No expectations. Just how you feel. It's way underrated with today's youth. Keep it simple, they need to tell the people they care about how they feel without all this use of computers, and all those smart phones. You go find that young man of yours and take his hands in yours, look him in the eyes, and tell him what's in here." She patted her hand over his heart.

"You're a very dear lady," he finally managed to say.

"You mean nosy." Her smile broadened once more, patting his hand with her own. "I am, but you mark my words, young man. Do as I say and you shall succeed."

"Okay, I've got nothing to lose." Kai smiled at her. "Thank you."

"Good luck. Remember, speak from the heart."

"I'll remember." He waved goodbye and watched her walk away, shaking his head as he chuckled to himself. With his focus back on Luca, his mood became serious. She was right, though. The only way to reach him would be to speak directly from the heart. To be honest, and hope he was willing to listen, and give him a second chance.

SECOND CHANCES

LUCA DRIED HIS tears with the bottom part of his T-shirt. He hadn't realized he'd been crying until he heard himself sob and, by the time he'd figured it out, he hadn't been able to stop. He still didn't get why he was crying. It was so stupid and lame, really. Luca jerked his hand over his face, drying the last of the tears away. He was even more pissed off now than when Kai had accused him of being gay.

How dare he! He was *not* gay. He wasn't... He stopped what he was doing, remembering earlier that morning and what he'd done while thinking of Kai. There was no explaining that, not even to himself. He'd played their conversation over and over in his head, trying to make sense of it, rationalize it, but hadn't succeeded very well. The things Kai had said scared him to the core, and he'd almost started to hyperventilate. Because nothing of what he suggested could be true! It couldn't!

He felt incredibly stupid for crying, but Kai's words had opened a forbidden door inside him he couldn't get to close back up. It didn't help that he wondered what his father would say if he came in and saw him. Thank God, his parents were gone for the day. That gave him plenty of time to get himself together.

What if he was wrong and Kai was right? Why did it scare him so?

You know perfectly well why.

Had Kai been right? Was that why he was so upset? But, he couldn't be right. If he was... No, he wasn't going there. He felt embarrassed by his lack of control and even though he tried to deny why he was feeling the way he did, he couldn't ignore the nagging voice in his head calling his bluff.

Kai had said things, things which made sense but to admit them, even to himself, would only cause him pain. Why did Kai have to see! Why couldn't they be like they'd been last night? It had been good then—fun. And he had been happy, it had been simple.

"You know exactly why you're feeling the way you do, but you're too much of a coward to admit it, even to yourself." His own words made him cringe. Was that really his voice? The words coming out of his mouth sounded raw, almost hateful. It was true, there were things about himself he never spoke about, things he never really let himself think about or permit to rise to the surface, because there was no point in doing so.

He was right! And you lied. You *threw him out because he saw in you what no one else has. The truth!*

Why, when his life was already mapped out, would he even bother with anything else? *To fight for yourself, moron!*

Yeah, that was easy to say to yourself, when no one was there to listen. His parents, especially his father, would never accept having a son other than the one he pictured in his head. They would still expect him to do what they'd planned for him—to go to medical school, become a surgeon. He could be anything he wanted as long as it fitted their plan for him, and didn't shame them. Marry the girl they approved of, drive the right car, have two-point-four children, with the house, and the dog that came with what they called the perfect life. True happiness was for the poor who couldn't afford to buy the fake kind, the kind that left you empty but kept up the appearances of a happy life.

Luca pulled his feet up onto the couch, wrapping his arms around his knees, feeling very alone and sorry for himself. There was a tight band around his heart; putting an ache there he didn't know how to undo. Part of the ache he'd put there himself when he drove Kai away. But mostly he felt upset that he didn't seem to have the backbone to be truthful or stand up for himself, less to his father. Weak, that was what he was, and God, it made him nauseous.

He could hear his father's voice in his head, telling him to suck it up, that life wasn't fair. He wished his father had been someone he could turn to and talk with, but he never had been and never would be. He let out another sob, the emotional turmoil going on inside him was something he'd been able to ignore, until he met Kai.

Oh my God, what have I done!

Only twenty-four hours after meeting him, everything had changed and boiled to the surface—all those things he'd buried deep down inside—inconveniently.

How was that even possible? Why now? Why Kai? He didn't understand. He only knew Kai was the reason, and it had been like blowing the lid off the kettle. Maybe Kai was right.

How long could he keep lying to himself and, foremost, why would he want to? Would it help him to be open and honest with himself even if it changed nothing? Luca felt scared, but maybe that was part of growing up, knowing something was real. That you felt the change the confession made. It wasn't like he had to go out and shout anything from the rooftops, right, but maybe admitting to himself would help him feel better? Isn't that the advice people gave you?

That the truth would set you free?

For the longest time, he merely sat there, his mind blank, trying to convince himself to say it aloud but nothing left his lips. *Say it! Open your mouth and say it. Admit it! It isn't that damn hard to say. Just say it!* Luca yelled the words into his mind, squeezing his eyes shut. *No, No, NO!*

"I am… I'm…spit it out already. How hard can it be!" He scolded himself, rocking back and forth, his breath hitching. Covering his ears with his hands, on his next breath he shouted out, loud enough for the words to bounce off the walls and back to a place deep inside himself. "I'm gaaay!"

It felt liberating. He did it again, letting his hands fall away from his ears this time. "I'm gay. I think I like boys… I mean men. God, no boys." He wasn't that twisted, was he? It was sort of hard to tell these days, where he was concerned.

The instant ease of the tension around his heart and mind was affecting him so much, he felt lightheaded. He took a deep breath, and then another, before opening his eyes and looking around himself as if the world was changing right before his eyes.

"I can't believe it, but I'm gay. It's kind of ridiculous how I didn't know, but I'm really gay," Luca whispered to himself repeatedly, trying to get this new realization about him to register in his mind.

He tried to swallow the lump in his throat but he was dry from crying. As he stood up, his legs were a little unsteady, shaking underneath him, making his steps wobbly like Bambi on ice. Running his fingers through his hair, he looked at the way his hand shook. By the way his body reacted, you'd think he'd come up with the solution to world hunger.

"Get a grip, Luca. This. Is. Not. A. Big. Deal. There are plenty of gay people in the world. You're not some sort of abnormality." To his parents maybe, but not to the rest of the world. Too bad his parents weren't the rest of the world. Walking through the grand hall, he saw his reflection in the large floor-to-ceiling mirror. Meeting his own eyes and what he'd freshly figured out about himself, hit him like a kick to the stomach.

"Oh my God, I'm gay!" He slapped his hand over his mouth, looking around, scared someone might have overheard him. He was gay. He liked boys. He had no interest in girls, whatsoever. He was gay...gay like...gay, gay. Like Jonas Gardell gay, the most famous gay comedian in Sweden, who was a floosy like RuPaul. He rolled his eyes, no way was he ever dressing up in women's clothes. No way, Jose. Zero chance.

Stepping into the kitchen, he poured himself a large glass of water and drank it like he hadn't had anything to drink for days, before refilling the glass. Leaning against the counter, he stared off into space.

Admitting what he'd done had lifted a huge weight off his shoulders he hadn't realized he'd been carrying. The more he thought about it, the more sense it made.

I do really like guys. I want them. No, I want him, I want Kai!

Wait! He put down his glass on the counter.

He wants me, too; he said so. I know he did!

His smile disappeared as quickly as it had appeared, not because of Kai but because of what had happened with him. More precisely, what he himself had done and said to him. He'd been so rude, and Kai had been right all along.

He had to find a way to get hold of him. Maybe it wasn't too late. He needed to say he was sorry; to tell him he was right. He might not know him, and he might not be anything but a simple flirt. Or, he may never see him again, after today's disaster, but telling him he was right still mattered.

He'd been pushed to face himself. He may not be a quick study, and there might never be a chance to live his life openly as a gay man—he doubted it, actually—but being truthful and honest to himself made him feel amazing. Snapping up his head, he turned the faucet on again and splashed his face with water before drying it on a towel.

Kai mattered, that was simple. He had to try to catch him.

Without giving himself any time to second-guess his decision, he pushed away from the counter in such a hurry he almost lost his balance. Luca's hands were still trembling as he picked up his phone and wallet, shoving them down into his pockets before running out the door.

He headed for the tram stop that was only minutes from his house; it was the most logical place for Kai to be heading. Luca had to stop running to take a few deep breaths. He was used to jogging but his mind was going a mile a minute and he wasn't getting enough air into his lungs.

Luca knew Kai lived in one of the student apartments close to the downtown area. At least, he could be downtown when, and if, he got hold of him. They could meet up and talk. Then maybe, if he was lucky, Kai would forgive him.

Fishing his phone out of his pocket, he tried to get his fingers to work and find Kai's number. Walking and looking down was never a good thing, especially for a klutz like him, but he ignored his own warning this once…and paid for it when he ran into someone. The hit was so hard he would have fallen over if it wasn't for two strong arms wrapping around his hips and catching him right in time.

"Oh, thank you! I'm awfully sorry…" Luca looked up to thank his savior properly but found himself speechless. The person holding him was Kai. He hadn't left! A wide smile spread across Luca's lips as their eyes met. He shouldn't be smiling, it was wrong, but he couldn't do anything to stop it. Right now, right here, was all that mattered, and Kai was still there.

He licked his lips, nervously. What if Kai was mad? What if he wouldn't listen? Why was he still there?

"I'm sorry!" They both spoke at the same time and burst out laughing.

"I'm so sorry, Luca. I never meant to upset you…" Kai said softly.

Luca felt Kai's hands moving on his hips, warm and solid against him.

"I'll go first. Please!" He put a finger on Kai's lips as he started to speak. "No. I'm sorry. I was so rude. I was scared, Kai. I'm still scared, but you were right. I was lying." He leaned in closer, speaking low but fast. "I didn't know I was…well, I did, in a way, but I didn't know, Kai. I'm sorry. I didn't mean to lie. Or be awful and mean. Forgive me!" He was talking a mile a minute, trying to get it all out to ease his heart and mind.

"You have nothing to be sorry about, sweet Luca. I was a pushy bastard, and I did what I always do, I assumed instead of asking. I'm the one who's sorry. Can you forgive me?" Kai looked up at him with regret in his eyes.

"There's nothing to forgive. What you said was right. All of it," Luca whispered, looking down at his feet.

His chin was tipped up with one of Kai's fingers; it felt warm and right against his skin. "Right or not, it wasn't my place. But I did want to help, that was the only reason I pushed as much. But, tell me, right about what?" Luca smiled as his eyes met Kai's. "I need it in plain English. Now I'm so scared of assuming something, so spell it out for me."

Luca wrapped his hands around Kai's arms and took a step nearer. He was standing closer to him than he'd ever been to anyone—boy or a girl—in public. But, for the first time in his life, he didn't care. His heart was pounding, he was nervous and scared, but somehow, it didn't matter right at this moment.

Luca's cheeks heated a little but he didn't look away.

"Right…right about me," Luca whispered, his eyes never wavering from Kai's. "I'm so scared, you know… I don't know what to do." He looked around, voice low. "I mean,

I'm like you, I'm...gay. My father, Kai...he will never accept it. I just..."

"*Shh...*" Kai said soothingly, rubbing his hands over Luca's arms, giving him a reassuring smile. "It will be okay. We don't have to figure all of this out now. You did a huge thing today, you admitted it to yourself. Do you know how brave that is?" Kai gave him a genuine, sweet smile. "I'm so proud of you."

Luca beamed back at him.

He felt euphoric, standing there with Kai, knowing he knew, as if he was floating. And, with that feeling, he did something he'd never done in his life. With a last, quick glance around to make sure no one was looking, Luca let his hands slide over Kai's shoulder. He squeezed gently as he watched his hands move over his body, loving how it felt—the awareness of muscle underneath the fabric of his shirt. With a deep breath, Luca leaned in to brush his lips, pushing a breath of air into Kai's waiting mouth.

Slowly, he moved his lips over Kai's in a sweet kiss, humming contently at the warm silky feel of Kai's lips against his own. He was surprised how good it felt, how fast his body responded to the simple touch, as Kai's tongue came to trace his lips.

He gasped, letting his lips part, flinching a little at the strange feel of Kai's tongue in his mouth. It felt foreign but not unpleasant. And, for a second, their tongues touched before he finally pulled away. Luca's legs shook again but for a completely different reason.

When the kiss ended, Kai leaned his forehead against Luca's and smiled. "Wow, that was even better than I imagined it would be."

Luca bit his lower lip and smiled like a fool. He could barely speak after their shared kiss, not to mention everything else that had happened. Taking a step away, he let his hands fall to his sides, instantly missing the contact but the reality of where they were had hit him. He couldn't afford to have anyone see them.

"Come on, let's go back to my house, and we can talk there." He nodded in the direction of his house, giving Kai a shy smile.

They walked next to each other and Luca snuck peeks at Kai from under his lashes. He felt so good right now, even if what he'd done and what it meant caused his stomach to tie up in knots. At the same time, he felt lighter than he'd ever done, relieved, almost. It was true; the truth did set you free, even if it did bring new obstacles.

There was so much left for him to figure out, and he had no idea how he'd go about it. But, maybe, if he was lucky, he wouldn't have to do it alone. He stole another glance at Kai who was looking straight at him. His smile broadened as their eyes met, making Luca's heart skip a beat.

There was no way he was telling his parents about this—they could never know.

He gave Kai another smile, one he hoped came off more confident and secure than he felt.

Concentrating on walking, putting one foot in front of the other, he pondered his choices. *Oh, for the love of God, Luca, for once in your life, live a little!* He did the second bravest thing he'd done that day and reached out to touch the back of Kai's hand with his own. He wrapped his fingers around a couple of Kai's and squeezed gently.

He could feel his gaze on him, it felt so good, so liberating, and it was bold to touch Kai like this. Luca felt good about it in the pit of his stomach. Looking into Kai's warm eyes, it was easy to ignore the screaming voice telling him to run.

The minute they arrived at his house, Luca closed the door behind them, shutting out the world as he stepped up to Kai, standing as close as he dared but not knowing what to do. The emotions inside him ran high with conflicting thoughts. He shouldn't, but he wanted so much to touch Kai. To feel his warm skin against his, to know how it felt to touch and be touched by someone who was as attracted to you as you were to them.

This was his first time he'd openly and freely admitted to being sexually attracted to anyone. He knew he wouldn't have many moments like this, and he wanted to bask in it. His breath came in quick, shallow pants as he took Kai's hands in his, placing them on his hips.

"Touch me." He breathed, his voice shaking slightly, as his heart pounded in his chest.

"Oh, I would love nothing else." Kai gave him a broad smile as his fingers pulled the shirt out of his jeans, only to let his hands slip in under the fabric and run up his back in slow, featherlight movements. Luca gasped at the instant spark of sensation tingling his skin. His flesh broke out in goosebumps, making him shiver with pleasure. Oh God, it felt so good being touched like this.

Mimicking Kai's movements, he lowered his eyes to the waistband of his jeans, pulling his tee up. Hesitating, he looked up to meet Kai's heated gaze. Kai didn't say anything, but gently kept his hands on Luca's lower back. It made him feel safe with Kai's strong arms around him. With a deep breath, he snuck his fingers under Kai's shirt, running the palm of his hands up his abs and chest.

Leaning his head forward to rest against Kai's, he listened to the small sounds of pleasure coming from him as he moved his hands more bravely over his warm skin. As his fingers encountered his nipples, all it took was a brush of a finger for them to perk up, seeking more of his touch. He did it again, slowly rubbing his thumbs back and forth over the little round peaks until Kai moaned into his ear.

"That feels so good, Luca." Kai's voice was a low, husky sound that made every hair on Luca's body stand bolt upright. "But if you don't want me to cream my jeans, you need to stop."

Luca couldn't help the grin spreading across his lips. "I make you feel like that?" He gave Kai a shit-eating grin.

"Yes, you do." Kai grinned back.

"Cool."

"Now, shut up and kiss me," Kai murmured two seconds before he made Luca's toes curl as their lips met in a warm, mouthwatering kiss.

STOLEN MOMENT

THE NEXT COUPLE of weeks went by in a blur. Luca and Kai spent all their time together. He was no longer alone or, rather, he didn't feel alone. For once, he understood the meaning of fun and school in the same sentence. Kai would sneak in with him to some of his lectures, sitting next to him, listening, holding his hand out of sight from others, of course. He was so adorable and sweet, giving him time to adjust. Never putting any pressure on him.

What surprised him the most about spending all this time with Kai was that he'd expected it to make him feel less, but it made everything about him feel right. Kai brought out something inside him no one had ever come close to. It was hard to explain what it was, but for lack of a better word, he felt brave and strong. It made him feel confident in himself, as if he could do anything.

It was only May but spring was being kind to them this year, and it was warmer than normal. It gave them the opportunity to spend their free time outside, Luca showing Kai the sights. One day, Luca took Kai to the amusement park and they'd ended up there all day, going on rides, eating junk food, feeding each other cotton candy, and laughing a lot. Like a lot a lot—it still made Luca smile like a fool thinking about that day he'd first squeezed Kai's fingers with his own. Looking down at their laced fingers, he realized they'd been holding hands ever since they stepped off the train.

They were in the small city of Varberg, located about an hour south of Gothenburg by train. Here, nobody knew them, and the chances someone Luca knew would end up in Varberg on a workday were slim to none.

Although, at that very moment, he didn't really care one way or another. He probably wouldn't say the same if he was caught, but he was flying. His stomach fluttering, heart soaring. Every time he looked at Kai and their eyes met, he felt like he'd won the lottery. Kai knew things about him no one else did, and that made what they had even more special.

"You having fun?" Kai's voice spoke low in his ear. It was heavy and gravely like he'd recently woken up, making Luca frown as he turned his head to look at him. What he saw in Kai's eyes couldn't be mistaken for anything but lust. Not even by a novice like him. Luca pulled in a deep shuddering breath, unable to let go of the hot stare.

He nodded, unable to speak. Kai smiled, as if he could see the effect he had on Luca and loved every moment of it.

"What has you thinking so hard, darlin'?"

Oh my God, did he just call me darling? Luca bit his lip to stifle a groan. Fuck him. He swallowed hard, eyeing Kai as he fantasized about him in his cowboy hat, boots, and the same tight jeans he was wearing now. Shit! He was getting excited. He had to stop. He felt the hot prickle as a blush crept up his neck and spread onto his face.

"Oh, now I really want to know what you're thinking." Kai let go of his hand, slipping his arm around his waist, before pulling him closer and guiding him to a bench in a small cove of the castle wall overlooking the ocean.

The pressure of Kai's hand on his hip wasn't harsh but the effect it had on him was like he'd been gripping him hard, hard enough to leave a mark. Luca squirmed, a soft whimper slipping from his mouth. His prick was pushing hard against the zipper of his jeans in the intensity of the moment. The vivid images of Kai gearing up in his mind, together with his emotions running haywire, he thought he might come purely from listening to Kai speak.

"Oh God," he whimpered, squeezing his eyes shut, sitting down abruptly on the bench. He reached down, grabbing himself through his jeans, squeezing hard, trying to stave off his impending orgasm. What, the hell, was wrong with him? Didn't he have any self-control? A soft chuckle made him open one eye and peer suspiciously at Kai.

"You think this is funny?" He heard the hurt in his voice but couldn't help it. Luca didn't like Kai laughing at him.

"Oh, darlin'."

He gasped at the endearment; there it was again. It really got to him. The endearment itself, and the way it sounded spilling from Kai's mouth with his twang. It was like being touched.

Kai sat by his side, leaning into Luca, one hand caressing his shoulders as the other lifted his chin to tip his face so they were looking at each other.

"I wasn't laughing at you, but if you could see yourself right now..." He didn't say anything else. Instead, his eyes roamed over him, drinking him in, making Luca's pulse beat heavily in his ears.

"How do I look?" Luca swallowed and whispered, unable to look away.

"Like pure sex," Kai said instantly, smiling. "You make me hard."

Luca watched as Kai's fingers circled the wrist of his hand in his lap, bringing it over and discreetly cupping the hard bulge in his jeans.

KAI WATCHED LUCA'S lips form a silent "oh," his eyes flickering between his crotch and face, cheeks delightfully flushed. He was stunning, eyes bright and alive. If they'd been anywhere else, with more privacy, he would have taken

Luca out and jacked him off. But, knowing Luca's predicament and not wanting to push him too far, he used every ounce of willpower to keep himself from doing exactly that.

Leaning in, he brushed his lips against Luca's, tongue flicking out to trace those plump soft lips, nipping gently.

"Oh God. I'm gonna come. Oh God, help me." Luca started to wiggle, looking at him with panic in his eyes. Doing the only thing he could think of to help Kai sat up and pulled Luca over so he was straddling his lap.

"What…what are you doing…? I can't…" He stuttered, eyes worried.

"*Shh,* I'll take care of you. No one will see a thing. All they'll see is your back and two guys kissing. Trust me," he said as his swift fingers plucked open the buttons of Luca's jeans and reached into his boxers to bring out his cock. Curling his fingers around the warm skin, he watched a pearl of precum on the red swollen tip, peeking through the tight foreskin.

He took his time, enjoying the moment, taking Luca in. His cock was long and slim, fitting his hand perfectly. He got a good solid grip around him, forming the perfect tunnel with his fist, making it easy for Luca to push through his hand's tight grip. He wasn't circumcised, which only made him look hotter in his eyes. From what he'd gathered, most Swedish men weren't, unlike the US, where most were.

Kai licked his lips, looking up at Luca's face into his blue eyes. They were lust-filled, his lips parted, body rippling in involuntary spasms. Damn, he was so fine like this; completely taken by his own lust, nothing else mattered, almost.

"Mmm…you're stunning like this, my darlin' Luca, and look at this." He tightened his grip around Luca's warm, rock hard cock, only looking away long enough to get another eyeful of his fine member.

"Such a pretty cock. Feels so good in my hand," he whispered, cupping his other hand around Luca's neck, pulling him in for a kiss. He meant to make the kiss a light brushing of lips, maybe a small swipe of his tongue to taste, but the second their lips met, his world was set on fire. He moaned against his mouth, eagerly swiping his tongue over Luca's lips, silently begging Luca to let him in. His hand moved over his cock in quick hard strokes, making Luca gasp. He mumbled Kai's name over and over, against his lips, before cupping his hands around his face to deepen their kiss.

"Kai... Kai..." His voice was low and hoarse.

The kiss was good, not very skilled but Luca was getting better. Besides, this was probably his first time being close to a man in this way.

A second of guilt rushed through Kai but Luca started to rut against him, making him forget all about feeling guilty.

"Oh...oh...God. I can't not move. I have to move...oh God," Luca whimpered, his hips making small movements, pushing up into his hand.

"There's no one here, only you and me. Let go, darlin'." Gripping his shoulders hard, Luca's eyes were wide, huge, staring right at him but he was gone completely in his lust. His hips snapped up wildly, repeatedly. Kai couldn't take his eyes off him, as his own hips rolled up and pushed up against Luca's ass to get some friction. He was going to cream his jeans if he kept going like this but Luca was so hot, so sexy, and he felt amazing. He didn't know if he cared.

Luca was so far gone; it looked like wild horses couldn't have stopped him from doing what they were doing. He moaned, pushing into Kai's touch. In the distance, he could see people approaching; they were going to be caught soon if they didn't hurry. The way they were rutting against each other, there was no way people wouldn't get it.

Making quick work of undoing his pants, Kai whispered urgently, "Come on, help me, darlin'. I need your touch."

Luca looked at him with dazed eyes. With a little help to push his jeans flaps aside, his cock bounced out of the confinement, thick and hard. Guiding Luca's hand to wrap around his shaft, he knew it wouldn't take a lot for him to blow. From the look on Luca's face, he was right there on the edge, too. With people getting closer and his own climax tumbling through him, Kai swept his thumb over Luca's cockhead.

Luca threw back his head, arching his back, throat working as he came. Cum poured out of him, spurting, landing on Kai's hand and arm. He loosened his grip some but kept stroking Luca through his climax.

"So fucking sexy. Fuck, Luca. You make me so damn hard. I'm right there, darlin', just need…"

Luca's lips crushing his, kissing him hard—almost wildly—silenced his words. Kai came with a loud moan muffled by their kiss, his hips snapping erratically as he pushed himself over the edge.

Opening his eyes, Kai found Luca watching him closely, as if waiting for his reaction. He smiled and, seconds later, Luca returned it.

"That was something. More than I expected." Kai panted softly, his hand still around Luca's flaccid cock, the other cupping his face, tracing his lips with his thumb.

"So fucking stunning."

Luca blushed a deep shade of red, wiggling in his lap. The people he'd seen in the distance were coming closer but far enough away to not see anything but the two of them cuddling. They were in Sweden; people couldn't care less about anyone being gay.

As they approached, he saw it was a group of four girls, a few years younger than them.

"Whatever you do now, my darlin', don't move, okay?"

Luca nodded, still smiling. He heard the giggles, Luca blushed even more, if that was possible, before the wolf whistle came. Kai thought Luca looked ready to dive into a hole in the ground. He looked mortified.

"Oh darlin', don't be scared." Kai cupped his cheek. "They didn't see a thing. They thought we were making out. Okay?"

Luca looked at him suspiciously but eventually gave him a nod.

WHAT WAS HE doing? It might not be the first time he'd ever kissed anyone but it was the first time he'd done anything like this, and his body felt like it was on fire. There were a couple of girls he'd kissed and fooled around with, but he'd never once felt like this. Here he was, sitting in a man's...in Kai's lap, in public and getting off! Jesus. He lifted his hand to run it though his damp curls.

"I wouldn't do that if I were you," Kai said, taking hold of his wrist, bringing it back down to rest on his thigh. He looked at Kai, then down on at hands, and there it was. The evidence of their...of whatever it was. He'd had sex in public. He. Had. Sex. In. Public. He couldn't stop staring at his hand. He watched as Kai carefully tucked him back into his jeans, fastening a few of the buttons.

"I'll let you do the rest so I don't get you all messy."

Kai was as damn messy himself. He started to slide off his lap, forgetting Kai was as exposed as he'd been moments ago. But Kai didn't say a thing. He tucked himself away quickly before bending down and wiping his hand on the grass, then zipping all the way up.

Needing some space to think, to get his emotions under control, Luca pulled down his shirt over the still loose buttons on his jeans and headed for the water to wash his hands. Walking straight toward the sea with determined steps, his eyes darted all over the place, the water, the rocks leading down to the ocean, there was a swan couple near the edge of the water, both white. Pretty—the swans, that was, he bet they were really at peace. They looked like they didn't have a worry in the world, he thought as he stumbled over his own two feet. He fell forward hitting his hand on a sharp rock and cried out in pain.

"Luca!" Kai called out behind him. He heard him move but was too preoccupied trying to get his footing back before settling for kneeling, holding his throbbing hand, trying to breathe around the pain.

There was a cut on his hand, about three centimeters long. From the looks of things, it was clean, but it was hard to see with all the blood. Oh God, he was getting nauseous. He could feel the blood leaving his head, making him lightheaded, and the noise around him sounded muffled in his ears.

I'm not passing out. I am not *passing out.* He chanted quietly to himself, barely noticing Kai crouching down next to him.

"Luca? Your hand. Oh, darlin', let me help you."

Luca watched him as if in slow motion, putting his jacket down next to him before unbuttoning his shirt, only to pull his tee over his head and wrap it around his hand.

"Oh." Luca inhaled deeply, eyes locked on Kai's chest, wandering down to his abs, only to wander back up, taking him in, inch by inch.

"Oh," he said again, sounding dumb, but he knew there was nothing else he could say. Kai without his shirt on was a beautiful thing. Distracted by his nakedness, the throbbing pain in his hand was merely a dull pulse.

Kai's soft chuckle brought his eyes back up to his face. He felt himself blush.

"I don't mind, darlin' Luca. I like you watching me, especially if it feels as good as that did." With Luca's hurt hand in his lap, Kai caressed his face with his hand.

94

"You could feel that? How…" He shook his head, not knowing how to relate to what Kai meant. He wasn't stupid, he got what he was trying to say but the emotion was strange to him.

As if Kai could read his mind, he ran his thumb over his lips. "Yes. Your eyes on me are as silky smooth as our lips, warm as your skin underneath my fingers"—his breath hitched in his throat and his heart started to flutter as Kai's fingers trailed down his neck—"and as arousing as your hand on my cock, stroking."

Jesus, if his hand wasn't such a mess and hurting like hell, he might actually have gone for a second round, right there and then.

Luca frowned, ignoring the aching need that, despite the pain, was making itself known in the pit of his belly. Being with Kai was starting to get dangerous. He said all the right things, and made him feel things he'd never felt before—things he didn't even know existed.

"Come on, darlin', let's get you to a clinic, get that hand looked at. Then, when you're all wrapped up, I'll take you for a nice long lunch somewhere, and we'll indulge in Swedish goodies."

Luca followed Kai with his eyes as he stood up, taking hold of his good arm and the elbow of the injured one. Thank God, it was his left one. His father would have had a minor fit if he'd hurt his dominant hand. It was going to be bad enough as it was, but he wasn't going to think about that now. He smiled at Kai when he helped him up.

"Now, don't move. Let me help you, okay? Let me grab our things." He made a joke about not letting him go as if he was going to fall over from standing still, which wasn't a complete impossibility. More often than not, he did have two left feet. He let Kai help him back up to the grassy area where they stopped once more to let Kai put his shirt back on. Luca let out a little disappointed sigh. It was a shame to cover up something so fine but he guessed it was necessary.

Kai looked up, eyes twinkling with mischief. "I promise to take it off again for you. Soon."

Luca felt his cheeks pinking up again, and he had to look away from Kai's intense gaze, but he did chuckle softly.

"We could go to the beach sometime. Do you wear a Speedo, too?" A wide grin spread across Luca's face, he felt brave for daring to tease back. It felt good to do so. Kai threw his head back, laughing hard.

"Come on, you cheeky one." Kai winked at him, grabbing his jacket in one hand and pulling him into his side with the other.

"I can carry it," Luca said, reaching for the jacket.

"Nah, I got it." Kai smiled, holding his hand out of reach. "You keep that hand up and elevated, hmm?"

It felt good, being taken care of like this; it made him feel special. The best thing was that, when Luca looked at Kai, it showed in his eyes, his smile, in the way Kai's body pushed closer to him instead of splitting apart when they walked through extra crowded places.

Slipping his good arm around Kai's waist, he let out a happy sigh, smiling, this was good. Despite his injured hand, he was having the best day of his life, so far.

ROMANCING

IT WAS GETTING close to the end of the semester and there were still too many group papers and exams to be turned in, as well as research to be done. Luca's father was on his case about not forgetting his studies, questioning him about his sudden time away. Luca didn't lie and told him how it was.

"Father, we're required to turn some of these tests in as a group and, frankly, I enjoy hanging out with them. They're fun."

His father had given him a skeptical look. "Fun. This is no time to have fun, Luca. You need to focus on your studies, becoming a surgeon is no easy task."

"Yes, Father, I know. But they have the same pressure I do. We're all pre-med, remember," Luca had replied quickly, meaning nothing by it.

"Don't get snappy with me, Luca. You will do as I tell you." He'd been silent for a moment, looking at him with stern eyes, exactly the way he always did. "Fine. But if I see one slip in your grades, one…" he emphasized the word, "you're cut off. You hear me?"

Luca had nodded, promising there wouldn't be a slip of any kind.

Most of his schoolwork with his classmates could, of course, be done over the net. Why do that, though, when doing it in person was so much more fun, especially when it included being with Kai. The best part was, Luca didn't have to feel guilty. Well, at least not more so. Other than hiding the reason why he was so eager to be with Kai—none of it was a lie. They did have fun in between the books. To be perfectly honest, they spent a lot of time in the parks on a blanket studying together and much less time in the library or school computer labs. He was studying, though, that was the whole point, right? He was happy, together they were in this perfect bubble, and he had a new friend. Life was good.

Luca's last class for the day was finished. A bounce in his step, he was moving faster than usual. He couldn't wait to see Kai; he was so excited, it made his stomach flutter.

They'd been seeing each other nonstop for almost four weeks, and it was perfect. Their trip to Varberg the previous week was something they both still lived on. Things had happened on that trip to bring them even closer. They'd gotten serious a lot quicker than he'd ever expected. But he didn't try to ponder it too much. Doing so only led him to feel hopeless and sad, because he knew his future didn't consist of him and Kai as a couple. He knew that much.

But, instead of their relationship getting less intense, the intensity was growing and becoming stronger. The more time they spent together, the harder it was not to touch, smell, and feel Kai at all times. The best thing he knew was to nuzzle Kai's neck, sliding his nose over the warm smooth skin there, breathing him in. It was intoxicating and arousing as hell. He smelled like a warm summer's day, mixed with soap. The mere thought of it made his heart skip a beat and his prick twitch.

On days like this, when life hadn't given them any time to see each other, not even for a quick lunch or coffee or simply to catch up for a few minutes, Luca needed to see Kai. He had to force himself to slow down, instead of running like a lunatic down the hill to Linne Street, where they were meeting up. He cherished every moment they had together and it was limited as it was. Together with Kai, it felt as if he could catch his breath for the first time in his life.

It still amazed Luca every morning when he woke up that he'd been able to come out. In a way, it felt like a dream, even if coming out in his particular situation was only to himself and Kai. He'd never really let himself think outside his self-imposed limits, like he'd done lately, but here he was, a month after meeting Kai, free in his own mind—well, at least freer. He wasn't planning to come out to anyone else.

This thing with Kai was only temporary; something to help him deal before he'd go back to how things had been. It would help him through the rest of his life when he fulfilled his parents' dreams and expectations. He'd have a really happy time to focus on, no matter how short it was.

Eventually, Kai would go home. To be more precise, he was going home in a mere six weeks. Luca dreaded the day more than anything else but he had six more weeks, to live and let live.

There was no point in ruining the time with worrying about the whys and what ifs. Life wasn't fair but at least it had given them both a window of happiness. He coped because he knew, when Kai went home, he was going to a family who loved him precisely the way he was. Soon enough, he'd meet his Prince Charming to share his life with, and Luca would be left with the memories to last him a lifetime.

Or so he told himself anyway.

Luca didn't spend as much time these days thinking about what it meant spending time with Kai and what others would think. He'd come to realize there was no way he'd be without Kai as long as he was in the country. He couldn't turn him down. It scared him sometimes, because he didn't know how he'd react once Kai finally left for good.

Picking up his pace, he was eager to get to their meeting place. They hadn't had privacy since Varberg. One of Kai's friends had some water damage in his apartment and had been crashing at Kai's place, so that hadn't been an option. It was a studio and there was no solitude. Besides, Luca wasn't sure he'd been entirely ready for what that might entail. What had happened at Varberg had been thrilling and left him wanting more, even if it had been completely out of character, he wasn't normally that adventurous. But, being alone with Kai in his apartment...well...

He did jack off thinking about Kai several times a day, though, before getting up and at night in bed. He touched himself in ways he'd never done before, exploring his body, imagining Kai's hands and lips on him.

He didn't care if they were in public and couldn't do anything but talk, even if his prick protested and wanted some alone time. All that mattered was spending time with Kai. Earlier that morning, when they'd texted before class, Kai said he had a surprise for him. He had no idea what it was, but it would be great.

He was meeting him at the Linnéplatsen tram stop; he could see the crosswalk from the top of the hill. He waved at a few people as he raced past, wishing them a good weekend, but didn't stop to talk.

Thanks to Kai, he now enjoyed conversations and spoke to several people on a daily basis. Not as special as Kai but he doubted anyone would be for a very long time. It had made him feel a lot better, both about himself and about going to school, though. He still wished he could study to become a vet but it was what it was.

Luca came down the hill and was about to cross the street when he saw Kai standing on the other side. He slowed down until he stood completely still, utterly taken with the sight as he absently pushed the crosswalk button.

Kai was leaning against the railing with his face turned up toward the sun. His eyes closed, a soft, contented smile played on his lips. He was breathtaking. Luca could have stood there all day gazing at him. So mesmerized by Kai's person, he almost missed the green light to cross. Because of the late start, he had to run across the last portion to make it in time. Still, a car honked at him to hurry the hell up.

The noise and attention it attracted made Kai open his eyes and look around until their gaze met over a few passing heads. The heated glint in Kai's eyes warmed Luca's insides, and his gut instantly stirred as it always did with him around.

Their relationship had grown from an innocent flirtatious friendship, to a very intense and intimate one in a short time. He knew it might sound corny and stupid, but it was as if their souls were connected. All they needed was time to flourish. Luca wasn't sure, but he'd bet a good chunk of money Kai hadn't expected that part either. They didn't talk much about what it meant, but he knew the longer they saw each other, the closer they came to having *that* talk. He didn't want to have the talk. It would mean many things would be asked—questions Luca had no way of answering, and expectations he most likely wouldn't be able to fulfill.

Pushing the unnerving thoughts aside, Luca walked up to Kai, so close their bodies were almost touching. He caught his scent, and oh, he did smell fine. Heat immediately flowed between them like an electric current.

"Hi," he said with a smile, his fingers twitching to reach out and touch.

"Hello, darlin'."

Luca's senses lit up at the endearment, a shiver ran down from his head and zinged right into his groin. He loved being called his darlin'. It might not be the most butch thing ever but it made him feel special. He wanted to be special. Kai's fingers brushed over his cheek and finally over his lower lip. Luca gasped, lips parting slightly at the intimate touch.

"How was your day? I've missed you," Kai said.

Luca blushed but he loved every word and every touch.

"It was okay, I guess, but it's so much better now. I missed you, too," Luca whispered and, without realizing it, pushed closer, wanting more of those magic touches on him. "A lot."

He pressed his cheek against Kai's touch, basking in the warmth of Kai's skin against his own. His eyes fluttered closed for a moment as he hummed happily. All he could think of was how much he wanted to touch him back. In the end, he couldn't help himself, the desire was so strong that need took over. Luca's hands skimmed over his naked skin, sliding up his arm, making Kai's flesh break out in goosebumps from the soft touch. The simple caress made his skin tingle and he could see from the darkened and dilated pupils that Kai was equally as affected.

It made him smile; he loved knowing he wasn't alone in feeling the way he did. In a flowing motion, without breaking eye contact, Kai's hands were on Luca's hips, pulling him in so they stood chest to chest, and Luca felt Kai's excitement poking his thigh. He swallowed hard, his Adam's apple bobbing.

"You make me excited, Luca." Kai breathed into his ear, leaning his head back an inch to smile at him as he brushed the side of his face. "A little bit more of this, and I'll probably cream my pants." He chuckled as Luca felt his cheeks redden. Burying his face in the hollow of Kai's neck, if only for a second, Luca breathed in the warm, dark fragrance known to him as "Kai." Did he do that? Did he make him excited? Was it possible for someone to care so much about him that a simple touch from him could have them wanting more? A lot more?

He leaned back to look at him. There was heat there in the pit of those eyes, a burning desire that could only mean one thing. Luca's heart leapt in his chest, as the burning passion in Kai's eyes made his own body respond in ways not fit for public. Luca's insecurities stepped in like clockwork, and he slid away from Kai's loving arms.

"I'm sorry." His voice muffled, but he took a deep breath before taking a small step forward, still touching but not as obvious, managing to arrange himself as discreetly as possible, his cheeks still rosy pink.

"Oh, don't be sorry. I love your hands on me. Never apologize for touching me."

The hard muscles of Kai's chest rose and fell, his breath slightly more exaggerated. Had it really been that...bad?

As Kai smiled one of those million-dollar smiles, Luca became so mesmerized nothing else remained, the traffic and people around them ceased to exist.

"Okay... Good... Um..." He stumbled on his words, but the smile on Kai's lips and twinkle in his eyes stopped him thinking altogether. He'd had no plans for what happened next but before he knew it, he leaned in and pressed his lips to Kai's. Luca could feel Kai's instant surprise. But, only moments later, his mouth latched on to Luca's, his tongue darting out to push his lips open. With a single gasp, it turned into the most mind-blowing kiss of Luca's life. The kind of kiss that made his toes curl and Kai moan.

He felt so brave and strong for daring to do what only a few weeks ago was unthinkable. Luca leaned all the way in against Kai, letting him take the full weight of his body, as he wrapped his arms around Kai's neck to get even closer and deepen their kiss. Luca had never felt a hunger like this before as his body and mind craved Kai.

He even dared to show Kai how much, by slipping his tongue in to lap against his, it was merely for a second but he did it. Kai moaned at the onslaught and he couldn't help smiling, while they still kissed. He'd done that, he'd made Kai make that little sexy noise, which must mean he was doing something right.

All too soon, Kai broke off the kiss, nipping once at his lip before pulling away. Luca made a sound of protest before opening his eyes and giving Kai a disappointed look. It made Kai chuckle and stroke Luca's hair out of his face.

"Maybe not the best place to continue this, huh?"

Luca looked around, as it dawned on him where they were, and how he'd been acting. Oh my God, he'd more or less been devouring Kai right there next to the tram stop. He tried to look around discreetly to see if anyone was watching but, as far as he could see, no one was paying them any attention.

Kai lifted his chin with his finger, and smiled. "Nobody is watching, Luca. Don't be scared."

"Yeah, maybe you're right." Luca gave him a sheepish grin. "So, what was your surprise?" He smiled and felt like he was bubbling over with excitement.

"Well, I was going to take you out for dinner and a movie, but how about we buy some take out, and go home to my place? Brandon got a call today, his place is livable again, I have my place back to myself. We can eat, talk, and cuddle on the couch, watching a movie."

Kai's suggestion was innocent enough but his eyes told another story. They were filled with desire, and his voice was still affected by what they'd done. It was filled with promises of more of what they'd shared. It made Luca shiver in anticipation and wiggle his hips from side to side, as if he was trying to get comfortable in his own pants.

Kai must have noticed because he discreetly pushed his knee between his thighs, grinding his groin exactly enough to give Luca some satisfying friction. Luca's lips parted at the sensation, leaving him to nod in agreement, sliding his hands over Kai's hips and feeling so bold, almost sensual.

They ran across the narrow road to catch the tram. Entering the vehicle, it was packed so they had to stand to the side in the corner but it didn't matter; they only had eyes for each other. Kai leaned against the car, pulling Luca close to him, and he willingly stepped into Kai's personal space, letting himself lean against him as he wrapped his arms around Kai's waist. He knew he was risking a lot. If someone saw them, it would go straight to his parents, but he couldn't not do it. It was as if someone else was running his mind but he wasn't complaining—he was loving every minute of it. After a moment of silence, Luca relaxed even more, there was no need for words.

He leaned his head against Kai's shoulder, enjoying Kai holding him. His own heartbeat drummed like crazy, from the thrill and rush of being like this with Kai and not feeling guilty, ashamed or scared that someone saw him. He watched the people on the tram, no one was looking at them strangely, and no one really cared. He met a strange woman's gaze and, for a few seconds, he thought he'd see disgust but she only gave him a reassuring smile.

A wide grin spread across his lips as he buried his face in Kai's neck. Kai's arms hugged him tight and he felt his breath ghosting his face as Kai leaned down to brush his lips against his cheek and nibble on his ear. The feel of Kai's breath and teeth on his skin made Luca instantly hard again, and he had to muffle a moan as he whispered into Kai's neck. "That is so not fair."

Kai's soft chuckle in his ear didn't help Luca get control of his raging hormones, but he looked up at Kai grinning widely at the mischievous look on his face.

It didn't take them long to reach their stop by Chalmers University. They slowly walked to Kai's apartment, not wanting to rush even if it was obvious to him that both of them were eager to be alone. They talked about school, their upcoming exams, how the rest of their day had been. The conversation flowed easily and Luca, for once, kept it going. Taking a detour, they picked up some Thai food, slowly making their way back to Kai's place.

KAI REGARDED LUCA tenderly. He was so proud of the brave man walking next to him. A man who talked vividly about his day. Kai looked down at their entwined fingers. He was oddly surprised how well Luca had adapted to his new self, and thrown himself into this new life wholeheartedly. It was wonderful but, at the same time, something told Kai Luca was trying to collect experiences. Not that there was anything wrong with that. Who didn't need memories, especially fond ones? They carried you through bad times, but what did it mean for them? Was Luca ever coming out and standing up to his parents? He wasn't going to worry about that now. Somewhere in his heart, he was positive if he only gave Luca time, it would all come right.

The man who clasped his hand so openly, showing his affection and desires was not the Luca he'd met, but he loved this side of him, being able to kiss him and hold his hand whenever the urge hit. Luca had come so far in so little time and was so brave. If Kai admitted it, he wasn't merely fond of Luca, he was falling in love.

He'd had a couple of boyfriends before but nothing that ever compared to what he felt for Luca. This was intense in a way going beyond some simple high school infatuation. It was the real deal, at least for him. Studying Luca as he spoke, there was a boyish smile and his big blue eyes shone in excitement. Kai adored the blush that was more or less constantly on Luca's cheeks and the smart, rapid mind that came up with the most fantastic thoughts and ideas. He loved all of it, like whoa!

He knew they were living on borrowed time, but it unfortunately didn't stop him falling in love. He was going back home soon. Kai told himself there was no point in falling for someone he didn't have a future with. If the distance didn't kill their relationship, Luca not being openly gay to his family or friends would eventually destroy what they had.

Kai knew he was lucky to have the love and support of his family, and obviously not everyone was that lucky. It didn't change the fact that his heart was in trouble, and he had to start protecting it, otherwise he was going to get hurt. But not now, he wasn't ready to let go quite yet.

He'd allow himself, allow *them*, a little more time to be young and in love. To live like they had forever and, maybe, who knew, maybe they would. Yet, deep down inside, Kai was hoping for a miracle of some sort to solve it all for them, so they could have their happy ever after.

Kai let his eyes linger on the man next to him, tracing the outline of his face and the plump, red lips curving into a smile as he spoke. He was beautiful and handsome, all at the same time, with soft features, not girly in any way, merely smooth and clean. Delicate. Kai loved how Luca fitted perfectly into the crook of his arm and was slimmer than he was.

Luca grinned and slid his arm around his waist, brushing his lips against Kai's, before finishing his story. Kai was lost in his lover's embrace, lost to his newfound belief in himself and the public shows of affection Luca gave him so freely. He had no way of shielding himself from Luca's newfound confidence. There was no point in pretending it didn't matter or that Kai was anything but overjoyed by this moment where they were like a real couple.

The dark cloud of what tomorrow would bring and how long it would last, knowing his heart would be broken into a million pieces, was still there. He couldn't deny himself this anymore, though. He was already lost to the feeling.

Kai didn't have the strength or will to fight against his attraction; he wanted whatever today and this night would bring in memories. Luca was his, and there was nothing else to say. He wanted him more than he'd wanted anyone else in his life, he wasn't going to let this chance of a happy moment with Luca pass either of them by.

With that settled in his mind, he wrapped his arm around Luca's neck and brought his head closer to kiss his temple.

"Okay, chatterbox, let's get us and that Thai food home. I want dessert after my dinner." He smiled knowingly at Luca, wiggling his eyebrows.

"What kind of dessert? Ice cream?" Luca teased.

"If it's offered from that pretty mouth of yours, then yes. But otherwise, more of those yummy kisses would do nicely." Kai laughed out loud at Luca's eager nod.

YOUNG PASSION

BY THE TIME they came back to Kai's apartment, they were both so hungry they more or less inhaled their dinner. Now they were half splayed out on the floor with pillows behind their backs, arms and legs wrapped around each other, classical rock playing softly in the background. The apartment was a studio, not very large, with the living room and bedroom combined, and that was okay. All Luca cared was that they could be together; all that mattered was the person beside him.

"That was good. I'm so stuffed right now; I don't think I'll be able to eat again for a week." Luca grinned, letting his muscles tense up as he stretched before relaxing back against Kai's warm body.

"You say that now. But in a few hours, you'll be asking, 'are there any leftovers, I'm feeling hungry.'" They both chuckled, knowing it was true.

"Do you want to turn on the TV and see if there's a movie playing? I'm pretty sure it's on the movie channel?" Kai said, rubbing his nose over Luca's hair, breathing him in.

"No. I'm fine." Luca shook his head, turning his face toward Kai so their eyes met, smiling shyly. "I like this, just us, the music…touching you. It's peaceful and…romantic." He gave Kai a crooked, shy smile.

They were alone and the anticipation of what was to come had them both squirming. The tension in the air was thick enough that you could cut it with a knife, and Luca was sure he heard it crackling like a fire getting a fresh new log tossed on it. He reached out, sliding his fingers down Kai's arm with a featherlight touch. The tip of his fingers seemed to sizzle like the air around them had been doing a second ago.

Luca could see and feel the effect his touch had on Kai. His body tensed and relaxed, the muscles rippled under his touch, and Kai's breath became heavier as did his own. He loved how, with a simple touch, he could get Kai's breath to hitch. It made him feel like could do anything as he continued his exploration of Kai's body.

Luca couldn't deny he was nervous. Not only was this his first time doing anything with a guy, aside from the kisses and crazy making-out touches, and that one mutual hand job they'd shared; but he'd never had sex with anyone. He was a virgin through and through, it made him swallow hard before nervously lowering his gaze, not wanting Kai to see the hesitation in his eyes. What would he think? Maybe this wasn't such a good idea after all but, God, did he want it. He needed to know how it felt to be with someone your heart desired—convinced it was the only time he'd ever feel like this.

"Hey, what happened, where did you go?" Kai tilted Luca's face up with his finger, forcing him to look at him. Luca's cheeks heated, but he lifted his gaze to meet Kai's. "Tell me, baby, what's wrong? We can stop if you want to. We don't have to do anything you're not ready to do, Luca," Kai said gently, brushing his fingertips over Luca's already sensitized skin.

"No, no...I...I don't want to stop." He got up on his knees, sliding over the soft rug and eased between Kai's legs, placing each hand on his thighs, moving them back and forth. "I want this; I want you...but what if I'm no good? I mean, I've never done it...at all..." He stopped, not knowing what to say. He felt stupid.

Kai leaned in, brushing his lips against Luca, pulling him up against him, forcing Luca to straddle his lap and place his knees either side of him.

"Luca, you couldn't do anything wrong, feel and let yourself do what feels right. Imagine what feels good, and that's what it will be. What you're doing right now feels really good."

He leaned in, claiming Luca's lips with his own, not giving him a chance to argue, only to feel. Luca gave in to the sensation of Kai's mouth moving over his, letting him lead. Kai took his time exploring his lips with his tongue, tracing them, tasting, and then letting Luca do the same, mimicking his moves. He nipped at his bottom lip, his tongue sliding against Luca's lips until they parted enough for their tongues to meet. At first Luca was hesitant, almost pulling back.

But as Kai kept exploring, relaxing, humming at the light touches of his hands, even Luca scooted farther up into his lap so their chests pressed against each other. The rhythmic drumming of their hearts beat against each other's as the heat between them increased.

IT FELT SO good, being this close to Luca, to feel his body pressed against his with nothing to stop them from exploring each other. There was a soft warning voice in the back of his head. Was he pushing too much, too soon? Should he be the one to stop it, before it got out of hand? But as the questions took speed in his head, Luca lapped against his skin, licking, kissing. As soon as he started sucking gently on his neck, all caution flew out the window. With his hands on Luca's waist, he pushed him down and bucked his hips up to grind against Luca's ass. There was nothing now that could make him give up this moment with his Luca. He was going to bust out of his jeans or cream them, whichever came first.

With one hand still on Luca's hip, he rubbed his other hand over the bulge in his pants, sliding his hand over, massaging Luca's hard shaft through his jeans. His blue eyes flashed with lightning heat, mouth falling open in a silent gasp at the simple touch. Imagine what he'd look like with Kai's hand wrapped around his length, stroking him from tip to root. He groaned at the thought and, if it was possible, grew even harder himself.

Luca's head fell back with a moan as he started rocking his hips into Kai's touch, needing more. Kai took every opportunity to run his free hand up Luca's side, bringing his shirt with him, managing to pull it up with one hand and shed it with some help from Luca.

Still rubbing his hand over Luca's groin, he kissed his way up his bare chest, tasting the soft sculpted body, breathing in the magnificent scent that was purely Luca. As he reached the sensitive spot between his neck and shoulder, he scraped his teeth along the line of his neck, making Luca press closer to him.

"OH...KAI, S'GOOD. Need more, touch me, please." The pressure building up inside Luca made him feel like he was going to explode. He barely knew what he was asking or what he needed. He only knew he wanted more, everything he was feeling was huge. There was too much and too little, all at the same time. God, he wanted skin, he needed Kai's warm and very naked skin underneath his fingers. He wanted to drive Kai as mad as he was making him. It was all crazy making, wonderful, and completely and utterly unhinged. There was nothing in his past memories that could measure up to what he was feeling at this moment. His body was on fire but the burn wasn't painful, it was delicately wonderful.

Cupping Kai's face in his hands, he dove in to a deep, hungry, messy kiss. The sound of their lips colliding seemed to echo in the room, bouncing off the walls, together with their grunts and moans. Luca wanted to taste every part of him, not only his lips but his neck, his chest. He ran his hands down over his collarbone to the ripped pecs, finding the hard little nubs hiding in a lovely carpet of soft brown chest hair.

He didn't understand where the emotions were coming from but it was all so huge. So big, he wasn't sure he'd be able to fit it all inside him. He wanted to devour Kai like he was the best kind of dessert till he withered in his hands. Luca eagerly tore at Kai's shirt and flinched at the ripping sound as he tried pulling it over his head. In the process, he tumbled over, ending up lying across Kai's body.

"Whoops. My bad." Luca chuckled, feeling high on love.

"You can say *that* again, but I'm not complaining. I love seeing you this eager."

Kai gave him a grin of his own, and tipped his head to the side as if he was studying Luca as he lay on top of him. Heated glances were exchanged, their hands moving in tandem over each other's bodies like they couldn't get enough.

Luca heard the small reminder of Kai's voice telling him to let go and feel—so he did. He slid his hands up over Kai's arms to follow the curve of those muscles. The temptation to taste them was a test of resistance; instead, he traced the lovely bumps of his arms. When Luca let them go to move down his body, Kai stretched his arms over his head.

Luca stopped moving, watching the feast before him, licking his lips. His prick pushed hard at his jeans, wanting out to rub against all that glorious tanned skin. Luca leaned over Kai, pressing their lips together in a hungry, sloppy kiss. Would he ever get tired of kissing Kai? What would he do when he no longer could?

He focused on his heart drumming in his ears, all his blood had left his head and was located in his crotch. Luca could no longer resist the urge to move his hips, rocking them in a steady rhythm, rubbing their denim-covered pricks together. He wanted to be loose and free from his clothes. Kai's lips were red and swollen after their kiss, his eyes hungry for more. Luca was sure he had the same, almost wild, look and he was fine with that, for he was free. He'd never been this liberated and he was savoring every second of this moment. *Come what may.*

Luca smiled as he leaned in to nibble at Kai's neck as he slowly moved down, tasting every bit of skin he encountered. Kai arched his back and moaned loudly when he flicked his tongue over his nipples, first one, then the other.

When Luca's lips and chin hit the hard fabric of Kai's jeans, he only hesitated momentarily before reaching for the button to unzip his pants, slowly. His eyes stayed on target, watching as the thick cotton-covered bulge popped free from the confinement of his jeans. Luca couldn't help licking his lips in anticipation, he really didn't know what to expect. It wasn't like he'd never seen a naked man before. But, it was different—a naked man in a locker room and seeing one like this, displayed in front of him, for his pleasure, was something completely alien.

His hands shook as Kai's dick twitched like it was fully aware of Luca staring, anticipating, needing, wanting, and being scared out of his goddamn mind.

"Luca…" He looked up, staring into Kai's warm brown eyes.

"No. I want to." It was all he said before he pulled Kai's jeans and boxers down over his legs. Beautiful and hard, he lay naked before him, his cock curving up toward his navel. Luca was so taken with the sight of him; he leaned back on his heels between Kai's legs, then bent and cupped the round fuzzy balls, letting the smooth orbs roll between his fingers in the gentlest of touches. *Oh God, the feel of them, it's like nothing I've ever touched before!* It was so good, it was almost like he could feel the touch himself.

Glancing up to see Kai's reaction, his lips were parted, tongue flicking out, and running over his lips, his eyes half closed. He was breathing heavily. He did it over and over, until Kai gasped, groaning loudly.

"Jesus, Luca...you're killing me here." His back arched like a bow before relaxing back down.

"I want..." He cleared his throat, cheeks flushed from heat and the shyness of asking, but he *had* to. "Kai, I want to taste you, can I taste you?"

"Please..." He begged, reaching for him.

Luca scooted back until he was lying flat on his stomach, Kai's hand landing on the back of his neck and shoulder. For a moment, Luca was so nervous, he almost froze when Kai's warm hand petted his head, pushing him to lean his cheek against Kai's thigh. So, he did and closed his eyes. For a minute, that's how they lay, Kai displayed naked—cock hard and aching for him—his own hard-on pressing into the floor and feeling like granite.

A million thoughts ran through his head—how good it felt to touch another man, how amazing it felt to caress Kai this freely. The feeling of strong confidence in seeing him aroused like this and that he had caused it was such a turn on. Luca wondered what he would taste and smell like. He placed his hands on either side of Kai's legs, supporting his weight so he could kiss his lower abdomen over his hip and down the inside of his thigh. He closed his eyes before burying his nose in Kai's groin, inhaling deeply, filling his lungs with the wonderful smell of Kai's sex, feeling his own dick jump at the scent of his lover.

The images of what he wanted to do to Kai's body played like an erotic movie in his head, making him rub his cheek against his prick and letting his mind guide him. God, he smelled so good. Soap, musk, and what Luca could only assume was Kai's own personal smell—it was heavenly. Luca kissed the inside of Kai's thigh again, trailing up to his other hip. Kai let out a disappointed groan when Luca bypassed his cock.

"Tease." Kai grinned and Luca gifted him with a sexy smile. Luca wanted to taste Kai so badly, it took every ounce of willpower he had not to take that perfectly bobbing cock into his mouth. He didn't because he was scared; scared of not doing it right. Luca had never given a blowjob in his life. How would he know what to do?

He kept watching Kai through his eyelashes as he slowly crawled up his other leg, kissing, licking, and nibbling on every part of his flesh, enjoying all the small sounds Kai made when he stroked sensitive skin with his tongue. When Luca once more, out of nervousness, kissed the side of Kai's shaft, but never fully licked or sucked him into his mouth, Luca felt Kai's hand on his head, guiding him toward the tip of his cock.

"Don't be a tease, Luca, please, suck me!"

Kai's cock brushed against his cheek as his face came as close as it could get without actually taking him in his mouth. He lost his own inner battle, not caring if he was good or bad, he wanted Kai in his mouth. Luca ran his hands up and down Kai's thighs a few times before taking hold of his shaft and giving it a few good pumps, watching a few drops of precum pearl at the very top. He leaned in, flicking out his tongue to taste those drops, and they moaned in unison. Needing nothing else, Luca sucked the plum-red mushroom head into his mouth. He slowly pushed his mouth over Kai's cock, taking in half his length before pulling away.

KAI'S HAND FOUND its way to Luca's shoulder, squeezing as he ran the other through his hair, holding his hand at the back of his head. He didn't push or force, he only wanted to show Luca he was there, because he needed the connection.

Oh God, if felt so good! How long had it been since he'd gotten a blowjob? A long-ass time, and he'd never had one like this. Yes, Luca's touch was slightly unsure, his technique not refined but it still felt amazing. He didn't need anything else but what he was getting. Luca's warm mouth wrapped around him was almost enough to set him off. Luca held on by gripping his hips as he bobbed his head up and down on his shaft. He was taking more and more of his cock in, getting eager, until he gagged when he took too much, too fast, and had to pull off, letting Kai's cock rest on his cheekbones.

"Feels so good, Luca. Mmm... Don't be shy, you're doing great. Trust me. Look at me." He chuckled; he was rock hard and aching. The thing he wanted to do to Luca was from pure hunger and from being turned on beyond what he could take.

"Yeah? You really think so?"

"I really do." Pushing up on his forearms, Kai kissed Luca lazily. His head spun from the lack of oxygen as their lips parted. Luca was back to teasing, licking, and nibbling, driving him insane with his mouth and tongue.

His hands explored on their own, touching his balls and cock, exploring every vein, bump, and texture. Kai was trying to be patient, knowing it was Luca's first time, so he lay there watching as Luca feasted on his body. He watched his tongue circle his nipples and suck them into his mouth. Unable to keep his eyes open, Kai's eyelids fluttered closed, his back arching into the touch.

The second Luca's face nuzzled his groin, he had to bite his lip, breathing deeply not to come on the spot. It had been a while since he'd been with anyone. Not that he'd had many lovers but he wasn't a virgin. First time or not, this was beyond any experience he'd ever had.

He held his breath as Luca's lips barely brushed the sensitive skin next to his throbbing cock. His hands reached out to tangle themselves in Luca's hair, guiding his mouth back to his shaft. He slowly rubbed his cock on the side of Luca's face, asking for entrance to the warm, wet mouth and, when Luca's mouth finally took him in, his eyes rolled into the back of his head with bliss.

He let his head fall back as he slowly moved his hips to the rhythm of Luca's bobbing head; the sensation of slowly getting to bury his cock into the heat of Luca's mouth was beyond amazing. Kai tried to not thrust too hard, he didn't want to make him gag and give him a bad experience. He wanted Luca to feel as if he was in charge and setting the pace. But, as his tongue once more swept over the tip of his cock and he sucked hard on the head, hollowing Luca's cheeks, Kai's body moved on its own and thrust deeply into Luca's mouth, his back arching with pleasure as he moaned in agreement.

Kai forced his eyes open to look down the line of his body, watching his prick disappear and reappear from Luca's mouth, finding it so erotic he almost had to stop watching. He nudged Luca's shoulder, forcing Luca to look up, letting his rock hard cock plop from his plump lips.

"What's wrong?" Luca looked so worried, his lips warm-red and swollen from sucking him. God, he was so sexy.

"Nothing. Nothing. Come here. I want to kiss you." He pulled at Luca's arm, making him half slide across his body, leaving a wet trail of kisses along his pecs and neck as he went.

With eager hands, Kai unbuttoned Luca's jeans, pushing at them and his underwear with his hands, tugging them down his ass and legs until they caught right above his knees. Not caring about it, Kai rocked up into him sliding his cock against Luca's. "I want us to come like this, cock to cock, rubbing together. I want to see your face, to look into your eyes."

All of a sudden, doing that, connecting with his lover, was more important than anything else, even getting off. The room echoed with both of the lust-filled sounds they made as their bodies touched from head to toe, rubbing hard together. Kai cupped Luca's face in his hands and hungrily started eating at his lips. Luca was quick to follow, eagerly returning the lustful kisses. Luca's hands raced all over his body, touching him everywhere, like he was unable to get enough of the feel of him under his hands.

Kai slipped his tongue in and out of Luca's lips, fucking his mouth in the same rhythm as their hips moved. His hands ran down Luca's ass, massaging the sweet bud between his cheeks. Luca threw his head back in a silent cry as his climax suddenly ripped through him and he came, spilling his seed between them, making the next few thrusts an easy slide.

Watching Luca climax, Kai let the fantastic sight push him over the edge, adding to their lovemaking, gripping Luca's ass, pushing against him, shuddering hard as he came. With a happy grunt and tight grip on Luca's butt cheeks, Kai rocked himself to completion, mixing his seed with Luca's between their bodies.

For what seemed like forever, neither of them moved. Luca's head was on his shoulder, his body still on top of Kai's and he wanted it no other way. Wrapping his arms around Luca, he held him as tightly as he could without hurting him or making him uncomfortable. He knew they had to get up eventually and shower, or at least wash off, but for now he was content and moving was not on the to-do list. Still holding Luca, he rolled them to the side, letting him rest his head on his arm, their eyes meeting in a warm gaze. Luca's eyes were shining and those wonderful, plump lips smiled sweetly.

"That was…wow…that was amazing. How I will ever be able to go back to jacking off, I don't know," Luca said, grinning as he slid a hand over his neck and shoulders, making Kai's skin break out in goose bumps.

"Maybe…you'll never have to," Kai said. His lips against Luca's, Kai playfully rubbed his nose against his before they kissed deeply without speaking another word.

IT WAS STILL dark when Luca woke up with a violent jerk. For a second, he was disoriented, wondering where the hell he was until he felt the warm body pressing up against him. He smiled, letting his eyes stay closed as he enjoyed the warmth of Kai sleeping soundly behind him, holding him tightly against his naked body for a moment longer. Luca turned his head a little and looked at him from the corner of his eye. God, he was such a gorgeous specimen and the way he was touching him, holding him protectively, made Luca feel so special.

Brushing his fingers over the sleeping face, Luca thought, *God I love you, you're so perfect.* Luca abruptly turned his head away, his cheeks rapidly turning hot and red, as a chill ran through his body.

No. No he couldn't, not love…no…

It wouldn't be fair, not to him, nor Kai. It could never be. What had he done? What would his parents say? They couldn't find out. That would be the end of this, the end of them, the end of life as he knew it. If his father found out about Kai, he wasn't sure what he'd do.

Love was not on the cards for them and yet, here he was, in love with his best friend.

Panic surged up in his body, and he had to get out. Now.

He squirmed his way out of Kai's grip, careful not to wake him. Luca didn't dare turn around to look at Kai as he crawled across the floor looking for his clothes and other belongings. He had to get out and away. He couldn't do this, he had to somehow erase this last part from his memory. It wasn't fair, not to Kai. He couldn't do this to him, what if he ended up falling in love with him, too? The pain.

No, he had to save him from that. For him it was different, he'd never forget. Kai would be the memory to last him a lifetime.

Luca didn't think, he only acted.

In sheer terror and guilt, he buried the beautiful experience he'd shared with Kai deep down inside himself. If he only got out of the apartment and away from Kai, all would be forgotten, nothing would happen. He could run home, sneak in, and no one would ever have to know.

He got dressed hurriedly, barely getting his shoes on his feet before he was out the door. His heart raced and his palms were sweaty, he needed air. He started to run down the stairs, he couldn't get away fast enough. Luca fell out the door and ended up on the sidewalk, shattered and confused. Tears fell down his face without him noticing. He started down the street with fast steps to put as much distance as he could between himself and that apartment. He had to get away.

He dried his face with the back of his hand and, the farther he got away, the less anxious he felt. Everything was going to be okay now. The words ran together. He repeated the words until he convinced himself that was the case. No one would ever know and later he'd explain to Kai why he'd left and Kai would understand. He always understood and everything would go back to normal.

THE FIGHT

LUCA WATCHED KAI as he sat next to him on the blanket with his laptop in his lap, typing away. His lips were moving as he typed as if he spoke the words before writing them. Luca leaned back on his lower arm with his books in front of him but after an hour he'd still only read about half a chapter. He blamed it all on the view and the amazing distraction Kai had become in a mere couple of months.

Without looking up, Kai smiled. "Why aren't you reading?"

Luca bit his lip before smiling, too. "Why read a boring medicine book when I have a stud like you to look at. It's so much more fun, and I love doing it." Luca blushed at his own words but he felt like he must be radiating heat and pure happiness. Kai gave him a small smile and went back to his typing. Luca frowned. He'd yet to talk to Kai about the other night, well, really talk.

Luca had asked if everything was okay and he'd said yes, but something was obviously bothering him because Kai was usually the happy, relaxed one of them. For the past couple of days, though, he'd been quieter and withdrawn. He didn't know what he'd done wrong, well, he did, but Kai had told him he understood. Luca had ended up texting Kai on his way home that morning, telling him he didn't want to wake him, but that he needed to go home before morning. He'd replied about an hour later that he missed him but he got it. Luca had been relieved. That was the great thing about Kai, he always understood, and that made all of this so much easier. But now, it seemed as if it there was still a problem. Luca felt confused, and scared at what it meant.

It wasn't easy to talk about how you felt ashamed for having sex with someone who obviously meant a lot to you, and that it couldn't happen again because it would destroy the people around you. It wasn't so much that he was ashamed of the act as he was conflicted and frightened of its implications.

How had he gone from cool, calm, and collected in a few short weeks to this...this...daredevil who loved a man openly? Well, not parading-him-around-town open, but openly in his heart and mind, doing it as if he had no cares in the world and free choice. But he really didn't have a choice, his life wasn't his own.

Even if he could deal with anything his father dished out, Luca was scared of what he'd do to Kai if he found out. Even the thought of anything bad happening to Kai—not that he thought his father would physically hurt him; it wasn't in him, but he could make his life miserable. Of all the things, he didn't want that. He knew his time with Kai was limited for more reasons than the fact he wasn't officially out of the closet. After a day apart, Luca thought there really was no point in him coming out.

"You sure everything is okay?" Luca said softly, barely audible.

Kai looked up, momentarily confused, but then smiled and nodded.

"Yes, Luca, everything's fine. I've told you. I do understand why you left but that doesn't mean I have to like it. This is...hard for me, too, you know, never knowing what's okay to do and what's not. But, yes, we're fine."

Luca cringed at the words but tried not to let on how badly they bothered him because all of it was true.

They had to be careful, no one could know about them or what they were doing. He didn't care too much about other students seeing them, none of his classmates had anything to do with his parents. But even if Gothenburg was a big city, it was still small enough that he could bump into someone he knew. He still had to think about what he did out in the open with other people around. Yet, at the same time, he couldn't help feeling a little offended by Kai's thoughts because often they'd been together, and he'd gone against what he knew he should do. They'd touched in public, he'd even kissed Kai for God sakes. More than once! Luca thought Kai was being slightly unfair.

It was a difficult matter and Luca had tried telling Kai. But his family accepted him and never expected him to be anything but himself. In Kai's world, true acceptance of one's person or demanding to be anything else but who you were and what you wanted to do didn't exist. Kai tried to be as supportive as he could, and tell him he didn't think his parents would react as badly as Luca thought they would. How could they since he was their son and all they truly wanted was his happiness?

He'd smiled at Kai because he sounded so convinced by what he'd said. How could he explain to someone who was raised with love and respect to understand expectations and obligations came before anything else? Especially something as trivial as being with the one you actually loved, if they didn't fit the expectations set out for you.

Other than Varberg, the other night with Kai had been his first real time having sex, not even a simple hand job. The one lousy attempt he'd had with a girl in high school was not even worth mentioning. The mere memory of it made Luca uncomfortable and embarrassed because he hadn't been able to get hard. He'd excused it as nerves and blown it off, not giving it much thought. It hadn't been until later when the thoughts of other men entered his mind more, that he started to doubt himself. He'd buried that deep within himself, never letting it resurface before meeting Kai. He knew he'd been living in denial, and still was to a larger degree, but he had no choice.

He looked back at Kai, thinking how much had changed for him in such a short space of time. How much he still had to explore about himself and them together, but time was running out before Kai went back home. As Luca realized what this meant, his smile slowly faded, he couldn't even keep up the charade for himself anymore. He'd entered into something that was doomed from the beginning, and it was tearing him apart. Glancing at Kai from under his lashes, he wondered if that was what had Kai so down, too. Or if he'd merely grown tired of the lies and limited relationship they had to have most of the time with other people around.

"We should probably end this, huh?" His words shocked him equally as much as he saw they shocked Kai.

"What?" Kai stopped typing and looked at him with a deep frown between his eyes. "End what, exactly?" Kai did a few more clicks, most likely saving his work before closing his laptop.

"Luca, what's the matter? Why are you so upset? Tell me." Kai pulled him firmly but gently into his arms and, for a brief moment, Luca let himself feel safe and at home in his arms. He leaned his head against Kai's shoulder and counted to ten—maybe it was twenty or even thirty—before pushing away.

"I can't, Kai. You know I can't," Luca mumbled. They were in the middle of the park and people were everywhere. Luca didn't dare look at Kai, he knew he was being unfair and, considering what they'd done the other day, he was a tease. But he was so scared.

"I'm being silly. Don't mind me, please. I'm okay, really." He dried his eyes with the heel of his hand and looked up at Kai with a smile. "I promise. I'm an expert in working myself up for nothing. I'm sorry."

Kai looked at Luca with a wrinkle between his brows and a hurt, worried look in his eyes. He didn't believe it for a moment.

"Stop saying you're sorry for everything, and talk to me, Luca. Tell me what got you so wound up and stop telling me it's nothing. I can see it isn't." He cupped Luca's face in his hands and kissed him very softly, a simple brushing of lips.

KAI KNEW SOMETHING was going on and had known it ever since the morning they'd spent the night together and he'd woken up to find Luca gone. He'd known even before he saw Luca's text that something was off. The not knowing what it was, though, had turned his stomach inside out, and he'd felt sick. He cared for Luca, more than he should, and he knew Luca cared for him, too, but it wasn't enough.

Luca's life, his parents it seemed, and his warped ideas of who he lived his life for, stood in the way of them really making a go of it. He could see the struggle within Luca, who tried to hide it, but when he looked into his eyes, it was so obvious. He was torn and fought himself on every brush of lips, touch of skin, and every emotion that had anything to do with feeling attracted to him. Luca still fought the idea of being gay, he didn't want to be gay, and he wanted there to be another reason, an excuse, for him to be sitting there with Kai the way he was. The days they had together were pure happiness, like the other day when they almost felt normal, were rare.

"Please, Luca; tell me why all of a sudden you're so sad. I don't want you sad. I'm here to listen and help but if you won't talk to me…"

"I WAS THINKING about you leaving and what it meant." Luca's voice was a mere whisper, the lump in his throat growing larger again.

"Things don't have to end with me leaving, you know. I can stay. You can come with me," Kai said with intensity, taking his hand and squeezing tightly. "You can come with me, go to a university in Texas and a veterinarian school."

Luca's eyes flickered between Kai's mouth and eyes as he spoke. What Kai said made his heart skip beats from joy. He wanted that. He wanted to follow Kai to Texas, to follow him anywhere he went; but he couldn't.

"I can't, Kai, you know that. I can't do that to them. They've invested so much time, money, and effort in me, I have to do as they say. I owe them that." He looked down at his hands, hiding his eyes from Kai's inquisitive gaze.

Kai's hand fell from Luca's face and he ran it through his long, wavy hair. He could sense Kai was annoyed but was trying hard to hide it.

"It's the way it has to be. This isn't real, it was …something to pass time, and we're friends. But it caught me off guard. I'm sorry. Let's not talk about this anymore, let's just have fun for a little longer. Hmm?" He tried to give Kai his most convincing smile.

Kai's entire body tensed. "Something to pass time…" he muttered, shaking his head as if he couldn't believe what Luca had said. His voice was colder and harder, as were his eyes when he looked back up.

"So, what are you going to do, Luca? Live a lie and be a gay man in a straight relationship? That sounds very healthy, and what about the woman you decide to marry and have children with? Doesn't she deserve to know what she signed up for?"

Deep down inside, Luca knew Kai was right, but it hit a sore spot with him, and the urge to defend himself was too strong. These feelings were all very new to Luca, and he needed time and space to figure out what they meant. And what to do with them. In his head he was both, he was the man he was with Kai, but he was also the boy his parents raised him to be; he couldn't let them down. Luca could feel the anger build up in him. How dare Kai sit there and judge him, make assumptions. He pushed away from Kai, who didn't stop him as Luca rose to his feet.

"It must be easy for you to sit there on your high horse and make assumptions about me and my life! They're my parents, they sacrificed a lot of things for me to be able to do what I'm doing. Don't you understand that? I thought you, if anyone, would understand, Kai, because you have a family and a family business, too. This isn't easy for me."

"Not easy for you, Luca. No, it isn't, and I get that a lot has happened in a short time, and I'm so proud of you. But not everything is about you, you're not the only one affected here. I have a lot invested in this, too, and to hear you speak of it as some casual passing-time thing…well, it meant…*no!* It means a hell of a lot more to me than that!"

"I didn't mean it like that. I'm sorry, but you want something from me I can't give you. I told you I can't be gay." He had to dig his nails into the palm of his hands to not start screaming, to keep his voice low so no one else heard.

"Luca, being gay isn't something you switch on and off like a damn lamp. It's who you are! Don't you get that?" Kai rose, stepping up close and putting his hand over Luca's heart. "It's in here and here." He tapped Luca's temple. "You can't change that about yourself, any more than I can."

"Well, I have to, and you have to respect that. I can't, Kai. I have to be who they want me to be. I have no choice."

He squeezed Kai's fingers, linked with his, the pain so obvious in his eyes. "Don't be sad, Kai. It's hard now, but in a little while, it will all go away and we'll forget. Before we know it, it'll be like neither of us ever existed." Luca meant it to sound comforting, that time would heal all wounds, but the tension in Kai's body and the pain in his eyes made it obvious that wasn't how he'd taken it.

"Yeah, I'm happy for you, Luca, that I mean so little to you that you can so easily push me out of your mind. Good for you." He snorted, shaking his head as he started to step away, his eyes filled with nothing but anger and pain. Bending down, he picked up his book bag, shoved his laptop in it and started to leave but turned back, looking at Luca with eyes dead.

"How the hell do you expect anyone else to understand or respect who you are if you can't respect yourself enough to be honest about who you are? It's beyond me. I thought I meant something to you! But damn, was I wrong, I was simply some experiment. What a loser that makes me, for really caring."

Luca took a step toward him and held out his hand but Kai held up a hand as he backed off. "Don't...don't touch me!"

Then he stormed off without so much as a backward glance.

KAI WASN'T THINKING about where he was going, too upset and angry to care. It felt as if his heart was cracking into pieces. He couldn't believe what Luca had said about what they were to each other, and how he'd, once again, taken everything back, changing his mind yet again. Mostly, he was in pain because Luca had more or less told him he'd regretted their night together, and that their entire relationship was a simple nothing.

It hurt for so many reasons. Kai didn't even know he could be in this much pain and still be standing. Someone he cared for, loved even, had denied his existence. All they'd been would soon be forgotten—apparently it was that easy.

How could Luca stand and look him in the eye and say what they'd had meant so little to him? Kai couldn't believe what Luca was putting him through; this was not the sweet, shy, and caring person he gotten to know over the past few weeks. As the anger started to subside, it was replaced by sadness and unshed tears. All his energy left his body in a single breath and he sunk onto a bench, fumbling around in his bag for his cell phone to call Kit who answered on the second ring.

"Hello, brother, what's doin'?"

It took Kai a moment to answer; it was all Kit needed to know something was wrong.

"Okay, spill."

"Hey. You got time?" It took Kai a lot to become distant and speechless. He had a temper, yes, and a tendency to storm off but usually that blew over in a matter of minutes. Then he'd come back with his game head on, apologize, or argue his case and move on. Now, however, Kai was breathing quietly into the phone, and Kit had to probe and pull to get him to speak.

"What happened, Kai? Talk to me, brother. Does it have anything to do with Luca?"

Kai let out a noise that sounded half laugh and half sob. Leaning his forehead into his hand, he let out a deep sigh.

"Yes, I guess it does. I don't know how you do it; how do you know shit like this?"

Kit chuckled. "Kai, for starters, you're not *that* big of an enigma and, secondly, you've spoken of very little else whenever we've talked for the past few weeks. So, what's the problem?"

Kai felt relieved his brother had exactly known what it was about, so he could get his annoyance and hurt out. He started from the beginning and told Kit about the conversation he and Luca had moments before.

"So...that's it. What do you think?" For a moment, he thought the connection had broken because Kit was so quiet. He had to say hello into the phone twice before Kit made a noise, letting Kai know he was still there.

"Wow, that was harsh. I understand you're hurt, Kai, I really do." He was silent for a moment, sounding like he was mulling over his next words.

"But…" Kai pushed.

"Do you think you might be pushing him a little too hard and expecting too much?" Kit took a deep breath. "I mean, what has it been, five, six weeks at most and, when you started out, he was in deep denial even to himself?"

That was so not the response Kai expected from his brother. He leaned back, running a hand through his hair, opening his mouth, only to close it again. Then he got angry and yelled into the phone.

"What, you're on his side now? I can't believe this, my own damn brother." Kai knew deep inside him that there was some truth to what Kit said, but that didn't make it hurt any less. It felt like it had been so much longer. Had it really only been a little over a month?

"So I'm picking sides now, is that why you called? For me to side with you and tell you you're right."

Kai grunted at his brother, thinking he was a traitor for turning on him, refusing to listen to sense and reason. But, of course, he couldn't help listening and, in his mind, giving Kit one more chance to turn it around.

But eventually he muttered, "No, I don't expect you to lie. But…" He wiped away a single tear threatening to run free.

"Look, Kai, I know you know that you acted on pure emotion because he hurt you. I get it. He denied not only himself but you as well. But, look at this from his perspective. When you leave, Kai, he has no one. You're the first person in his life that he felt comfortable enough with to be his true self. Do you understand what that means?"

Kai hated his brother for always being so damn reasonable, but it was what he loved about him, too. He always had the ability to see what was beyond all the emotions.

"Not only does that show the person you are, who could bring that out of him, but it also shows how important you are to him. He's willing to sacrifice everything he's been taught about who he is, and what's expected from him to be with you and be who he truly is with you, for whatever time you have together. What more can you ask of him?"

Kai didn't say a thing at first, what could he say? What Kit said hit home but he didn't want to admit he'd done wrong and rushed off, pissed off and agitated. He'd left Luca to fend for himself with a lot of demands from him, only because he didn't see the hardship Luca was going through about not being openly gay.

"Kai?" Kit's voice was softer now. "This might not be what you wanted out of your relationship, but I'm sorry, brother, we don't always get what we want. I've told you before, you've been lucky and blessed with Mom and Dad. Not everyone has parents who accept their kids for who and what they are. What we have is different, we take it for granted and don't quite understand how it can be any other way. But you know, as well as I do, that this is the way it is."

Kai let out a deep sigh of defeat. Kit was right and he knew it. However, it didn't make it hurt any less.

"Okay." He breathed. "I hear you, sort of."

"You're too emotionally involved with him to see it. What he needs is you to be there for him, no matter what, without the pressure. If you can give him that, I'm not saying that you could or should, that it's probably what he needs."

Kai nodded, as if Kit could see him. He understood what his brother was trying to tell him. In a matter of weeks, Kai had managed to alienate Luca twice because he didn't stop and think beyond the obvious.

"Kai, I can hear you thinking all the way over here. Spill it."

Kai narrowed his eyes and snorted at his brother.

"You're such a cocky bastard, Kit. If you were here, I'd punch you. But you're right and I've got to fix this, again. I hate that I get so angry and see red so that I lose it and miss the important stuff." Kai rubbed his hand over his head in a frantic, almost panicked, manner.

"Fuck, Kit! What do I do now? I mean, I know it's only been a few weeks but, damn it, he means something to me! He's not some random fling." Kai picked his book bag up and started back. Maybe if he was lucky, he'd still find Luca there and he could apologize, explain why he acted the way he did.

"I know this, Kai. To be honest, I'm worried about you. I'm even worried about him. You're leaving in a few weeks, and he's not in a place where he can promise you anything. Honestly, Kai, if he's set on pleasing his parents, what do you think you're going to be able to do? Maybe you need to let it go, for both of you."

"What? You've spent the last fifteen minutes telling me I need to ease up and now you say this. What the fuck, Kit? You're giving me as much whiplash as he is." Kai stopped walking, completely stunned by what his brother had said. He didn't want to think of what Kit was saying but still forced himself to ask. "What do you mean? Should I let him go and not talk to him again, not even to apologize?"

Kit kept silent for a little while before answering.

"That's not my choice to make, Kai. I know it's not fair, but you have to come to terms with what actually *is*, and decide what you're able to live with, and, most of all, what you can't live without. But maybe giving you both a few days apart is not a completely off-the-wall idea."

Kai sat down on another bench, feeling like he was losing it. This was so not the way he'd foreseen this conversation going. It wasn't the way he'd seen Luca and himself going, either. He thought they had more time, and that the other night had brought them closer, giving them both more of what they really wanted. That it had reassured Luca Kai was for real; and what they had was, too.

"Tell him the truth about how you feel but that it might be better for both of you not to see each other again…" Kit's voice trailed off. "That's at least what I would have done. I know it's not easy but, really, Kai, what are your odds of this working out? Maybe you're setting both of you up for more heartache than it's actually worth."

Kai sat there in the middle of the street with people walking by him, feeling isolated and alone. He wanted to run to Luca and pull him in his arms, tell him everything was going to get better, but did he actually know that for sure? Or was Kit right about setting them both up for false hope?

"Look, Kai, people don't always behave rationally when emotions are involved. Sometimes they open their mouth and garbage falls out. You know Luca better than I do. Do you think perhaps he was overloaded and said the first stupid thing that popped out of his mouth? I'm not saying you don't have a right to be upset, but this has to be monumental for Luca."

Kai sighed. "I know…" he reluctantly agreed. "Kit, I'm going to have to call you later. I need to think."

Kit gave his brother a few last encouraging words and said he was only a phone call away, come day or night. Kai grunted in return and hung up. With a heavy heart, he backtracked his steps and headed for home. This day had gone from complete joy and relaxation to the worst day in his life. How was he going to walk away from Luca?

Massaging his temple, all of a sudden he was struck with a headache from hell. He was lost on what to do, knowing there was some truth in what Kit said about them being in two completely different places in life. Neither of them knew if they'd ever get to the point where they were both on the same track. Hell, considering the conversation they'd had back there, the odds of them ever being able to have a normal relationship were unthinkable. Where did that leave either of them, and where did that leave him?

Kai hadn't admitted it to Kit, he was sure he knew, though, that Kai was so close to falling head over heels in love with Luca. After today, Kai didn't think Luca felt anywhere nearly as strongly for him. The only thing Kai knew was that he had to get to Luca, but he didn't dare go to his house again, in case his parents were there. Whatever happened, he didn't want to out Luca by mistake or get him in trouble. At the same time, though, Kai couldn't leave; he had to say goodbye.

THE HONEST SON

O N HIS WAY home, Luca tried to tell himself Kai would be back, that he'd be running after him soon enough. Luca had even slowed down his steps as he walked toward the tram stop and, purposefully, he'd missed the first few trams home because he didn't want to miss him. He knew he'd hurt Kai and that he needed a little while to calm down. Luca sat there on a bench telling himself Kai would be there, but no matter how long he waited—he never came.

Eventually, Luca realized he wasn't coming, that Kai had chosen to walk away from him forever.

Luca sobbed as he got on the next tram to take him home. He was lucky enough to find a single seat in the front where there were fewer people. Luca needed to be by himself and, most of all, he didn't want anyone to see his tears. He was heartbroken, devastated over what had happened and what he'd done. But he didn't see how he could have done it any differently. He only wished he hadn't left Kai with the impression that what they had didn't mean a thing to him—when, in reality, it meant everything.

He looked out the window and hated the sun for shining and the people on the street for smiling and laughing when he wanted to lie down and cry his heart out. He wanted it to rain, so he could stand out on the street crying as the water drops cloaked his tears.

He knew he wasn't getting his wish, though, so he dried off the tears that escaped his eyes before they even fell to his cheeks, knowing that between now and home, it was all the grieving he was going to get. He had to get a grip on his mood and his sorrow before he saw his parents, especially his father. Otherwise, he'd start to ask questions, which would force him to lie, and he hated to lie.

He'd had enough lectures for a lifetime, especially after the other night when he'd come home at six in the morning. Everyone simply *had* to know where he'd been. Luca had lied and said there'd been a group of them watching movies, and he'd passed out on a couch. His father believed him, but had given him a half-hour talk about priorities.

His dad was, and always had been, a non-emotional person. Luca couldn't remember his father ever being impulsive or casual about showing his emotions toward anyone, not even to Luca. He couldn't remember the last time his dad hugged him or treated him like his son with no demands or expectations.

He let out a deep, hitching sigh, his mind drifting off, and he thought of Kai. Would this really have been their last time together? How had it gone so wrong, so fast? One minute they'd been sitting there and everything had been fun, calm, and relaxed. Five minutes later, all hell had broken loose. Luca knew he was mostly to blame, but he'd panicked and, instead of telling Kai he was scared of confronting everyone he knew and coming out, asking for help—he'd pushed him away.

It amazed him how comfortable Kai was with himself and his sexuality. It made him almost jealous of how secure he was with himself, too, and that people would accept him for who he was. Those who didn't, he easily shrugged off their attitude and opinions, like water off a duck's back.

Every time Kai pushed him about coming out in the smallest way, it made Luca panic. He did what all cornered animals do to get away: they bite and scratch, and do pretty much anything to get free. That's what he'd done, and it had cost him everything. He never meant to hurt Kai or deny what or who he was. It only came out on pure instinct. Luca hadn't even been honest with himself about his sexual orientation and he was only now getting used to being this way himself. He wasn't ready to be outwardly gay toward others, yet.

He leaned his head against the cold glass of the tram window. How could he have said to Kai that it had been nothing more than a way to pass time? It wasn't; it never had been, from the moment they'd met. He didn't mean it, not then, not now, not ever. But he'd been so pressured and put on the spot, torn between what he was supposed to do and what his heart told him to do. Reason, surviving, was so deeply rooted in him, there was no room for a gay son in his parents' plans.

Kai's last words haunted him. *If you can't respect yourself enough to be honest to you, then how can you expect others to respect you?*

It was an honest question, a question he had no answer for. Nor did he have an answer for what he'd say to the woman he'd one day marry. How would he explain not feeling any passion? Would he be able to fake it every so often, when he knew what heaven tasted like? Would she know he never really loved her? Maybe, if he was lucky, he'd meet someone like Jessica who he could talk to, who could be his friend. Then, maybe, it wouldn't be so bad.

But that was way in the future—a future he didn't want, a future someone else created for him. Never before had he felt this much anger toward his parents, and chiefly his father, as he did in this moment. *Why can't we be a normal Swedish family, where the goal is to be a good person and happy? Why? Why? **Why?*** His mind screamed. He sobbed aloud, covering his mouth with his hand, turning away and closer to the window to hide his face from the world.

But the more he thought about it, the more upset and angry he became with himself. His complete lack of backbone was embarrassing. How was he ever going to become an independent adult if this is what he was going to do every time someone challenged any of his parents' wishes?

But he knew he didn't have it in him to go home and tell them the truth. He sank farther down in his seat. If he told them the truth, it wouldn't do one damn bit of good. In the best of worlds, he'd get a raised brow and a "really, how interesting" look, with "You've got responsibilities, Luca." That would be the end of that conversation. Luca was not a strong, self-confident, and "fight for your rights" type of person, he was a "do as you're told and everyone will leave you alone" person.

He shifted in his seat and once more turned his gaze toward the world drifting by outside the window, fiddling with his hands in his lap. Maybe this was a good thing, the fight with Kai, with neither of them going after the other. Their relationship was never meant to go anywhere, for more reasons than one. Kai was going to go back home to Texas, and Luca was going to finish his studies in medicine. Then he'd marry a good girl and have the life that was expected of him. He nodded to himself, this is what's planned out, and he wanted to please his parents, right?

He pulled the cord to signal he wanted the next stop.

As he walked home, he kept his head down and put his headphones on, in case he ran into someone he knew and whom he didn't want to talk to. He kept telling himself how good this break was. Of course, since he and Kai had gotten along so well and connected, it would take him a week— *okay, maybe two*—before he'd feel like his normal self again. *There was no other way for this to end anyway, it was hard losing friends*, he nodded to himself. Of course, it was, but in the long run, Kai would simply be erased from his memory and, in years' to come, Luca would only remember fragments of the short meeting with the American cowboy who he once knew. This wasn't a big deal, more a random thing, it was fun as long as it had lasted.

Sighing deeply, he huddled into himself. If that were true, why was he feeling so completely lost?

* * * *

LUCA STEPPED INSIDE the hallway and hung up his coat before kicking off his shoes. He could hear his parents in the dining room talking. He really didn't want to go inside and have to sit with them, have dinner, do the normal "tell me about your day" charade. He'd be expected to give a full report of his school day and after that came the advice, the lectures, and—if Luca was lucky—the "I'm proud of you, Son," but that wasn't a normality. As long as he behaved accordingly, that is what he got, no more, no less. Luca forced himself to plaster a smile on his face and step into the dining room.

"Oh, there you are, darling. I was going to give you a call and see where you were. Dinner is ready. You look a bit unwell. Are you all right?" Luca's mother smiled as she stroked his hair back and gave him a kiss on the cheek.

"I'm fine. Just tired." He brushed her off.

"Come have a sit, Luca, and tell me about your day. How did your test go? And why are you home so late? I thought I'd find you here studying when I came home." His father pointed at the chair that was Luca's, and he took a seat.

"I met up with a friend in the park and we studied together. The weather was so nice, so…" He shrugged. He didn't want to talk about his day with Kai at all.

"Mmm, a *friend*, what kind of friend would this be?"

He studied his father's face, he could tell he was upset, more than upset, judging by the red color rising from his neck, infusing his face. Luca frowned as his heart rate increased. What had his father heard and from who? He swallowed hard and tried to keep his emotion in place as he frowned up at his dad, raising a brow at the weird way he'd pronounced "friend."

"Ah, some guy from school. He's American, here for a semester doing his thesis. Why do you ask?"

His dad was obviously annoyed because he narrowed his eyes and snapped at him. "Are you being snotty with me, Luca? In case you are, I suggest a major attitude change!"

Luca opened his mouth to say something but closed it again. He was so confused; apparently, he'd done something that set his dad off but, for the first time ever, Luca had no idea what. There was no way in hell he knew about him and Kai, or what they'd been doing. There was no chance, was there? He opened his mouth again to ask exactly what he'd done when he felt his mother's hand on his shoulder.

"What in the world's name, Anders, has gotten into you?"

He didn't answer right away but kept looking at Luca, his eyes flashing with anger.

"Why is it that when I come home after a long day at work, I have to deal with getting phone calls about you sitting in a goddamn park letting some boy kiss you, Luca? Care to explain that to me? Because there is no way in hell any son of mine is gay!" He was yelling now, pointing a long finger in Luca's face. From the look of it, he was about to explode if he didn't find a way of calming himself down.

Luca could feel the panic rising, and his head was spinning at the information his dad had. How could he have been so stupid to be with Kai in public and not have figured out someone would eventually see them? He'd become too relaxed, there had only been a couple times where he let himself go. Oh God, he was so stupid! What was he going to do now he'd been caught? Was his life going to be ruined? He looked at his dad, scared out of his mind, not saying a word.

"Luca, darling, what's your father talking about? Did you let some boy kiss you?" His mother was looking at him as if she was seeing him for the first time. Her face was expressionless but her stare bore into him like a burning fire.

"Luca, didn't you hear me?" his father barked. "Explain to me why the hell you were letting some *hick* stick his tongue down your throat, and please tell me that's all you've been doing! You will be getting tested! Do. You. Hear. Me? Tested. Goddamn it!" He pushed his chair back, most likely to get his doctors' bag to draw the blood himself.

Luca shot out of his chair as his dad passed him and met his mother's eyes. They were sad, as if she knew something Luca didn't, or knew what he knew and like him denied it all. Luca ignored her by looking away and going after his dad to try to calm him down.

"Dad, please, it's not what it looks like, I promise. Who ever saw me with Kai apparently didn't look very closely because…" He was racking his brain to come up with something believable. Luca remembered Kai telling him about how his mother had breast cancer a few years back and how scared they'd all been, but now, six years later, she well again, the cancer in remission.

"Please, will you please listen. There's an explanation, okay?"

His dad stopped so suddenly, he almost ran into him. Luca had to take a few steps back to talk to his dad without feeling like he'd slap him across the face with his piercing look.

"So, explain." His voice was ice cold and completely devoid of any type of emotion. Luca knew he had one shot in convincing him that whoever had called him had seen nothing but an innocent hug between friends. A man giving another man a comfort hug, because his mother had been sick with cancer. Luca knew this was weak and lying like this was not only the wrong thing to do toward his parents but it was so disrespectful to Kai; he had no choice. The words came out before he had time to change his mind.

"Dad, Kai is three thousand miles away from his family. He's feeling homesick and was low, so yes, I hugged him. Maybe it was a little longer than normal but he was upset. What was I supposed to do, not give a shit because we're two men?" The lie fell so easily out of his mouth and, as he felt his own anger rush through him, it was easy to justify it. Who the hell called someone's parents because they saw someone kissing? It was so fucking stupid, and it proved what idiots the people his parents called friends were. His father raised an eyebrow at Luca's outburst and crossed his arms over his chest.

"So, you mean to tell me that Lars lied earlier? One of my oldest friends, who I've known for twenty-five years, called me up and lied to me about my own son. Why would he do that, Luca?"

Of course it had been Lars Gunnarsson, his father's closest friend. He was such a bitter old goat of a man, and now obviously a homophobe. Luca knew he'd always hated him for some reason and, seeing him with Kai, he had the perfect opportunity to ruin his life forever. He wasn't only a bitter homophobe, he was against everything and everyone who wasn't like himself.

"I'm sorry, Father, I know Lars is your friend and all, but he's a bigot and a bully." Luca didn't know where he got the courage from, but all of a sudden he'd had enough of the rich snobs, and snotty attitudes where he lived.

"You offer him your pinky and he takes your whole arm, and you know this. How can you believe anything he says?"

Luca's mother gasped as she came up to stand next to his father.

"You should know better than to act recklessly, Luca. We have taught you all your life that people make it hard to forgive, and impossible to forget."

He really was alone in this, neither of them really cared for him—Luca Von Bergendahl—the person.

He looked at his feet, shaking his head in disbelief. Why was he doing this? Who was he doing this all for? He'd been neglecting himself and his own wants and needs since, well, forever, and he honestly got nothing back for it, absolutely nothing. He thought about Kai and what he'd told him so many times, about lying to himself and what it did to him. He'd given him up, pushed him away and hurt him to be the son they wanted him to be, and this is what he got. The one person who had shown him kindness and liked him for who he was, was gone. And here he was, continuing that lie, all for nothing.

"Luca, I'm still waiting for an answer. I'd like you to explain to me why I should believe you!"

Luca couldn't help it, he let out a snort and then started to laugh, not for long but he did laugh. *Maybe you should believe me because I'm your son. Maybe you should support me, no matter what, because I'm your blood!*

"You find this funny!"

"The fact that I'm your son isn't reason enough for you, Father. You'd rather take a bitter old man's side, than your son's, no matter if he's right or wrong. I mean *that* little to you!" He was done and he was fuming. Before Anders had time to say anything about his poor attitude, Luca grabbed his new confidence and decided to set his dad straight once and for all.

"Luca, what on earth's gotten into you?" His mother exclaimed.

He didn't bother answering, what was the point. He could see what Kai had meant about being seen and why his words had hurt Kai so much, because denying himself had been denying Kai. He'd done to Kai what his father had been doing to him his whole life. But, no more.

"Father, you know what, fuck it! I've had it with both of you and your high society bullshit!"

The look on his mother's face, as he turned to stare at her with all the disappointment of her failing him, must have showed in his face. Hers was frozen in pure shock.

"Everything I said about Lars is true, except one thing. He was right, he did see me kiss another guy, and he saw me kiss Kai. He's amazing and the one person in my life who accepts me for who I am and demands nothing but what I can and want to give him." It felt so good saying it, to see the shock and anger in his parents' faces, at least there was a reason for it to be there and he'd put it there willingly. If admitting to himself who he really was, was freeing, admitting it to his parents was the ultimate liberation.

Luca took a step toward his father, and Anders actually took a step back.

"Hold on to your horses, Father, because your picture-perfect-son is in love with another man."

Anders opened his mouth to speak, his eyes dark and face bright red.

"Oh wait, that's not even the best part. Know I went down on my knees to suck his cock, and you know what, I loved every goddamn moment of it!" Luca knew he was pushing it. He could see by the look on his father's face and the hands fisting at his sides that one more push and he'd push back at Luca.

"Luca!" His mother yelled out his name so it boomed through the room.

"Oh just shut it, Mother!" He was on a roll, why quit now? "I've known I was gay since I was fourteen years old. No, I've known since I was fourteen, that I was different. I never once said the word gay out loud to anyone or myself, doing it all for you. To be the son you could be proud of!

But it doesn't matter what I do. You always spit in my face!" He pointed at his mother without bothering to look at her. She was the one who hurt him the most by merely standing there, not doing anything to come to his defense.

"I've been forced to ignore who I am to the point that I actually believed it myself. Kai is the best thing that has ever happened to me, because he helped me see who I really am and showed me that being me is okay." Luca was breathing hard and that was the only thing you could hear in the room.

"You have never told me that, not once, gay or not. I rejected the only person who ever really gave a damn about me, to be the person you wanted me to be. But, no more! I'm done."

For an instant, the room was completely quiet. You could hear a pin drop. His father was so angry and upset; he couldn't speak, refusing to even look at Luca. His mother was sobbing, covering her mouth with her hand.

How the hell could he have lived like this for so long? Well, he wasn't doing it any longer, he was done with wasting his life on them and their wishes.

He started for the stairs leading up to the second floor. He'd pack a few things and he'd go to his Uncle Soren who lived about forty-five minutes south of town. His father's brother, they never really saw him because he was nothing like them—he was normal. Hopefully he'd be willing to take him in for at least a little while. When he came to the first set of stairs, he turned around one last time.

"Oh, and while we're doing this whole confession thing, I might as well tell you, I hate, absolutely hate, medical school. I don't want to be a surgeon. So, I'm going to drop out and do what I've always wanted to do, and that's becoming a veterinarian." Then he walked up the stairs.

Not even when his father found his voice and yelled after him, did it occur to him to stop.

"Luca, don't you dare walk away from me! Come back down here! You will finish school and do as you're told! No son of mine is ever going to live a dirty life! Do you hear me, Luca!"

Luca heard his father's angry tone as he rushed up the stairs but he didn't care. He felt so light, so free, and he had no idea how he'd managed to say everything he'd wanted, in one breath.

This day had been the worst day of his life and in some strange way, the best.

Luca was so done living his life for others. His head was pounding, he was so tired, so damn tired of fighting, hiding, and feeling confused. He didn't have the energy to do it anymore. The first thing he wanted to do was to reach Kai and tell him about what he'd done, about getting out from under his father's thumb.

This, if anything, would prove to Kai he was serious about being with him, and that he cared. He only hoped he wasn't too late. He pulled out his phone from his jeans pocket, scrolling the screen to find Kai's number. The phone started to ring as his heart beat like a drum in his chest in anticipation of hearing Kai's voice on the other end.

SAYING GOODBYE

KAI LOOKED AT the unsent email he'd written. It was addressed to Luca. Simple and to the point, all he had to do was hit send but for some reason he was finding that extremely hard. It wasn't a huge surprise; saying goodbye was meant to be hard, right? If it hadn't been hard then it hadn't been that important to begin with. At least, that was what Kai figured from where he sat waiting at the Gothenburg Airport.

Kai had decided to say what he felt and leave it at that. After today, he was never seeing Luca again anyway, so he had nothing to lose. It had taken him a couple of days to sit down and actually start writing the letter. Saying goodbye was never easy but this had been the hardest thing he'd ever had to do. It seemed so easy in movies and books to bare your soul, but doing it for real was a completely different matter.

Telling someone who denied you that you loved them and wished them well was hard. It was impossible not to feel gutted and betrayed, instead of finding a solid way of letting go.

He'd turned his phone off so he didn't have to keep hearing all the incoming calls. Luca was trying to get hold of him but he didn't have it in him to talk face-to-face, or tell him over the phone. Kai knew the minute he heard his voice he'd be putty in his hands. His need for Luca was greater than his need to take a next breath. It was funny how some things became so clear when you were heartbroken. The sun set and the dark clouds parted, feelings blossomed, not making your life easier but breaking whatever part of your heart was still intact, crushing it into pieces with unrequited love.

Kai had spent a lot of time talking to Kit over the past couple of days and in the end he'd decided leaving was the best thing for him—for Luca, too. He couldn't deal with the heartache of losing Luca again and again, because he was scared his parents would find out about him being gay. Kai understood, at least he thought he did. It was a hardship for Luca, but at the same time he had to look out for himself, too; that was what he was doing now.

Right or wrong, the thought of never seeing Luca again, even if it meant only having him as a friend, tore at his heart. Kai was dying to hold on to what he could, but he knew walking down that road would only lead to more heartache. What he needed was to let go. To say he'd never forget was dumb but he knew, with time, the pain would cease and eventually Luca would be a cherished memory. At least, that was what he was hoping for. Kai didn't think he could ever completely forget Luca, no matter what.

They say that time heals all wounds—he could only hope that was true and with time, and the love and support of his family, Kai's heart would hurt less. A memory of something good, a person who once meant something great. Someone who'd left his mark on his soul as Luca had done.

He could learn from this—make it a lesson, to guard his heart better. Even back when they met some weeks ago, he'd had reservations, but he'd pushed them out of his mind, and everyone knew that out of sight, was out of mind. But, even if he wanted to, he couldn't regret meeting Luca. How could he? Luca was perfect, if not for this one thing.

The shy boy had blossomed in their time together, pushed himself so much and come a long way in accepting himself, but not enough to take the final step. Kit had been right; maybe he'd been expecting too much, too soon. Maybe he wasn't meant to be Luca's forever or even for right now. Perhaps this was some sort of twisted and warped love story that was only meant to carry someone through the rough patches of his life. Would he merely be a brick in Luca's house of completion?

He sighed deeply, running his fingers idly over the keys on his laptop. In the end, maybe he could find someone else to love, who loved him back. He sat there, playing with the laptop mouse, moving the cursor over the screen. Trying to force himself to send his farewell and get it over with, mentally girding himself for the moment it would become a reality.

You know it is better pulling a bandage off quickly than slowly. Do it.

However, he didn't listen to his own advice; he kept sitting there, staring at the blinking cursor. What if he was taking the easy way out? He knew Luca liked him and wanted to be with him. Kai saw it every time he looked into his eyes, and all those touches hadn't been a lie, he knew that much. He always felt Luca's eyes on him but sometimes, he'd let him study him in peace and pretend he hadn't noticed, because he knew how hard this whole situation of "being gay" was for him.

He only wanted to be happy, and Luca to be happy with him. He let out a deep sigh as he imagined Luca's ocean-blue eyes smiling at him; they were the most amazing eyes he'd ever seen. Sometimes, they'd watched him with such intensity, he'd felt the effect of his stare all the way down to his toes. One of those looks could make Kai grow hard in a matter of seconds. How many times had he fantasized those eyes on him as he'd been getting himself off?

The past few weeks had been the best in Kai's life. He realized writing the email that he'd never felt this strongly for anyone. Luca was not the only one who was a virgin. Kai was, too, when it came to truly being in love, which was why saying goodbye was so hard. It felt as if the second he pushed the send button, a part of his life he really didn't want to give up would be over.

But Kai knew in his mind, even if his heart wasn't on the same page, he was doing the right thing. Kit hadn't said much when he'd called to let him know he was coming home early; he didn't have to. He'd known Kai needed his family's support to get through the heartache, leaving Luca like this.

Kit had helped him arrange flights right away so he could concentrate on writing his email. He'd asked Kit if he was being a chicken for doing it this way and not telling him face-to-face? When Kit had said no, he asked how he could be so sure.

"Kai, you're in an impossible situation, you're hurting, he's hurting. You're leaving in a few weeks anyway, and he's not giving you any indication he's about to jump ship for you. To be honest, are you willing to stay in Sweden and take on that fight of trying to convince him he's gay? If he's not willing to fully admit to himself, what can you do?" Kit's voice had been warm but his words were full of truth as always.

He knew Kit was right, but it still hurt and it felt wrong to send him the email and go, but he saw no other way, he had no other option. He was scared to leave; he was scared to stay. Mostly, Kai was scared the pain that would come from leaving would scar him forever when the reality came crashing down on him and his heart actually caught up with his mind and understood Luca was gone forever. It would be too much for him to bear and he'd break down.

Kai hadn't realized he was crying until he automatically lifted his hand to dry off the tears falling down his cheeks. He seldom cried but these past weeks with Luca had been intense. Now it was too late, and he had to get out so he could start the process of healing and forgetting. For that, he needed to go home.

He'd managed to get out of his lease early since the demand of student housing was so high, and he'd had till Monday to vacate but he only had a suitcase, a carry-on bag, and his backpack so he'd already packed up. He'd left his apartment and turned in his keys the day after his last meeting with Luca. He didn't want to spend another minute in the apartment that reminded him so much of some of the best moments in his life.

Instead, he'd spent the past couple of nights on his friend Erik's couch. This morning, he'd written a quick thank you note to Erik; they'd talked the night before and said their goodbyes.

The cabbie who'd pulled up was about the same age as his father, he was friendly and chatted a little as they drove toward Landvetter Airport. Kai felt like he'd filled in all of the correct answers on America and his visit to Sweden. The last part of the way they'd thankfully rode in silence and Kai's thoughts had gone to the unsent email. He knew once he'd gotten through check-in and customs, he'd have time to send the damn thing. He couldn't leave Sweden without having sent it.

He'd leaned his head against the cold window of the cab, closing his eyes and sighing deeply. He'd felt so damn conflicted inside, he'd wanted to scream out loud, tell the world to stop spinning. One minute he was so sure he was doing the right thing but the next, he wasn't. As they'd come closer to the airport, the lump in his throat grew larger, the tight feeling in his chest becoming so intense, he'd felt as if he couldn't take another breath.

"Are you all right?" the cabbie had asked when they'd pulled up to the drop-off zone. The man had a concerned frown on his face and a hand on his arm.

He'd tried to smile. "Yes, yes of course. I'm fine. Thank you."

The man hadn't looked very convinced but he'd patted his arm as they got out of the car. Kai thanked him for his help and gave him a good tip.

He wished Kai well and bon voyage. As Kai had turned to leave, the cabbie turned back to him and handed Kai a small medallion.

"Take it. In my country, Turkey, it is called a *nazar*. It will bring you good luck and keep you safe from evil." He gave Kai a small smile and a last squeeze on the arm before getting into his cab.

Kai had looked after him as he left, brushing his thumb over the small blue and black eye on the front of the medallion. The small gesture from a stranger had made Kai smile and briefly feel a little better. It had been nice one stranger could see another stranger's pain and not be completely oblivious to it. Kai wasn't a person to hide his emotions. His mother said he carried his heart on his sleeve, and if he felt something, everyone knew about it.

He'd collected his bags and walked toward one of the check-in counters. Sleep hadn't been his friend last night so, as he'd stepped up to the counter, he'd only mustered a good morning and half smile, the angst of the unsent email weighing heavily on his mind.

He'd sat down at the Espresso House with its free Wi-Fi and ordered a large, black coffee. Kai said "no, thanks" to anything to go with it, he really wasn't that hungry. As his laptop had fired up, he'd rubbed his clammy hands on his thighs. The email had still been there, staring at him as if to say "are we still not done?"

To give himself a few more legitimate minutes to dwell, he decided to read through what he'd written one last time.

Dear Luca,

I have been sitting here for hours trying to find the right words to say to you, to not make you feel guilty or sad. I don't know if I'll ever find the right words, but what I've got to say is this.

First of all, I'm so sorry for how I ran off the other day in the park, and left you hanging. It was wrong of me to do that and even more wrong to not go after you. I hope you can find it in your heart to forgive me for being so selfish and scared. It took a lot for me to come to this decision. Letting you go is by far the hardest thing I've had to do, and to do it like this, with a simple email, breaks my heart. I know you deserve to hear it from me face-to-face, but, Luca, I have no other choice because if I see you again, I'll never be able to let you go.

I know it's not fair, I know how hard all of this must be for you, too, and how much you have had to accept about yourself in such a short time since we met. There's no room in your life for me, and I can't live with being someone's secret or being maybe a fling on the side when your real life allows it. I wish it didn't have to be like this for either of us, and that I could take your pain away, all of it!

But know that not doing so, not seeing you, makes me ache in places I never thought would ache, from missing someone. The past month and a half has been the best in my life. I will never regret meeting you, I'll never regret falling in love with you, and I'll only ever regret never getting to be with you longer than I did.

I want you to know that I'll never forget anything about you or how good you felt in my arms, or how special it was to be your first of everything. I had wanted to be your last, too.

Be happy my Luca!

Love always,
Kai

Without another thought, he pressed the send button, and the email was gone.

Kai's heart hammered in his chest and he asked himself what the hell he'd done. He'd poured his heart out in that email, hidden nothing and actually laid it all out there. It made him vulnerable. Picking up his coffee with a shaky hand, his mind still churned, and his body pumped so much adrenaline it made him twitch. He sipped the hot beverage slowly, letting his racing heart calm down. As he started to feel a little calmer and the first shock of sending the email started to subside, he realized he felt relieved.

He'd wanted to do what he'd done; it was a weight off his shoulders. He needed to bare his soul to Luca and let him know exactly how he felt. Kai had wanted to tell him for a couple of weeks now, but something in his gut had always stopped him. There had always been that small, and clear part of his mind that knew this wasn't going to last, because how did you have a relationship with someone who didn't even want to admit he was into guys; you couldn't.

After sending the email, he packed up his laptop. He had no more use for it and wasn't interested in seeing a reply, at least not now.

Instead, Kai sat there drinking his coffee and letting his thoughts drift for the time left before boarding.

He picked up his phone to call Kit, to make the time go by quicker but put it back in his pocket. Kai didn't have the energy at the moment to talk to anyone. Instead, he paid for his coffee and headed for the bookstore to find something decent to read for his fourteen-hour flight.

He smiled as he thought of the Kelly Ranch and his parents and siblings. He'd be coming home to the smell of hay and horses; he chuckled to himself as he realized he'd even missed the smell of manure. He merely shook his head at that thought but at least he was laughing, right? Yeah, some cattle shit and a home-cooked meal would make him feel better.

Kai browsed but couldn't really find anything until he came to the last shelf where there was a nice box set with all of the Chess Series. They were the same books Luca had been reading that day when Kai had surprised him at home. He pulled the box down; he had to have it. Kai hadn't known too much about the books before he'd seen Luca reading one of them. He'd looked them up later and they'd sounded pretty decent. He took the box to the cash register, paying whatever price they asked. This would be his one last connection to Luca. Those books would be the one thing he'd allow himself to have to remember him by. That, and the amazing photo a young man had taken of them when they'd gone to the sunny city of Varberg.

With the books clutched to his chest, Kai walked to his gate. Right as he got there, boarding started, the timing couldn't have been better. His thumb brushed the plastic box holding the books neatly together, like they could feel his every touch.

Carrying the box in one hand, he reached into his backpack and pulled out the one and only photo he had of him and Luca together. They were on the beach promenade, his arm around Luca's shoulders, and Luca had both his arms wrapped around Kai's waist—no inhibitions at all.

Kai had later sent the picture to himself and printed two copies, one for him and one he'd given to Luca.

Now he took the picture to bookmark the first page of the first book. Before closing the book, he brushed a finger over the side of Luca's face.

He was brought back to reality when he heard them calling out his section of the aircraft to board. He picked up his backpack and started for the boarding line. As he handed the check-in staff his passport and ticket, he turned around and took one last look out toward the airport as if Luca was standing there, and he wanted to say his last goodbyes. With that last glance, he started the long walk down the jet bridge toward the plane.

It was time to go home.

CATCH AND RELEASE

LUCA HAD TRIED to get hold of Kai for days but only gotten his voice mail. At this point, he was anxious and worried. The tension at his house was almost unbearable, and not helping him in any way.

His mother had come by his room this morning with a cup of tea, a fake smile on her face. She'd tried to "make him see reason" by telling him how wrong his life choices were, and that his father and she cared, or they wouldn't be trying to help him to better himself. He'd cut her off, told her to save it and get out of his room. He could see how much that affected her, but even if he felt bad for hurting his mother, he couldn't be bothered listening to any more of her hate.

Now he was standing there, watching the rain pound down on his window, feeling utterly relieved in one way and horrified in the next.

But what scared him wasn't what he thought it would be since meeting Kai. He thought his worst fear would have been facing his parents' judgmental hate. No, that had only been a huge relief, to finally see them for who they were.

What scared him the most was never seeing Kai again. That somehow, in his warped mind, he'd managed to push the one person who meant the world to him away, because he'd been so focused on his silly boyish fear of his father.

So, he'd told his mother what was on his mind.

"Mother, I am who I am. I know you don't like it, you've both made that abundantly clear. I'm leaving today so you don't have to have anything to do with me anymore. I'll go quietly so you can tell people whatever it is you need to tell them to save face."

She left his room sobbing, not saying another word.

He'd finished packing the little belongings he had, the ones he actually cared about. The picture of him and Kai taken on one of their excursions out of town, his Kindle, laptop, phone, and some of his clothes were really all he wanted, or needed. He looked around his room. There wasn't anything he wanted; it belonged to the other Luca, the fake one created to please his parents.

He'd called his Uncle Soren the day before, but hadn't told him much of what was going on, purely begged him to let him come and stay with him and Aunt Marie. His uncle hadn't hesitated even for a second. Instead, he'd offered to come and get him right away, but Luca had declined, wanting to give Kai as much time as possible to get back to him.

Soren was the real father figure in Luca's life, and he should have gone to him the minute he'd started his relationship with Kai. The thought had never entered his mind, though; that he had a choice. Why the hell hadn't he realized sooner? What he'd done the other night was something he could have done a long time ago, gay or not. So, why?

He needed the advice from the man who had been there for him throughout the years without ever judging.

It worried him that he hadn't been able to get hold of Kai, and he racked his brain for ways to find him. He'd gone by his apartment, but each time there was no answer. He must have been at a friend's house. Luca was going to call every single one of them he knew and see what he could find out. But, first, he had to get out of this house.

To get his mind off Kai, he thought about his parents. His mother had come up again, making some half-lame attempt to talk to him, but Luca's dad hadn't shown his face at all. Which kind of surprised him. His father never let an opportunity to yell at Luca go past. But the house was silent, as if everyone had left and he was the only one there. It was bound to be temporary, though.

He picked up his phone to dial Soren but got a busy signal. It made him think of how different his dad and uncle were. Soren had once told him he'd left home at eighteen because he couldn't stand his father's strict ways; he'd hadn't been an easy man to live with.

According to Soren, Luca's dad was a walk in the park compared to his grandfather. As a boy, his dad had been shy and he had adored his father, exactly like any young child. Luca's grandfather had taken his son under his wing and taught him everything. Soren had been rebellious and told his father more than once what he could do with his demands on how Soren should live his life. Soren said the only reason his grandfather hadn't kicked him out of the house was because of Anders who had looked up to his older brother. Soren had been the only one to get Anders to try things, open himself up, and relax when he was scared or nervous about things. Soren and Anders' father had realized that if he wanted Anders to follow in his footsteps, he needed to keep Soren around.

Luca knew from conversations with his uncle that he felt guilty for not seeing or understanding how much their father had influenced Anders. But by the time he'd understood where things were headed, it had been too late, and Anders was no longer interested in listening. He thought his brother had been a massive asshole. That's when Soren had packed his bags and left. He cleaned out his savings and headed to a friend in Stockholm, the only friend Soren had who wasn't a high society snob and whose parents had been more than willing to help Soren out while attending university.

The Stenmans had taken Soren in as one of their own. They'd lived in Gothenburg for many years and knew of his parents and had heard a lot about Soren's dad. Even though they didn't judge, they couldn't say they'd agreed with what they'd seen or heard about how the von Bergendahls treated their sons.

They didn't let Soren "pay his way" but told him to save and invest his money for the future, which he did. He'd spent the next five years at Stockholm University, studying business, accounting, and stockbroking. It was the only thing he'd inherited from his father; a head made for business. Soren invested most of his money and, over the years, he'd managed to turn what he had around and triple his investment.

After he graduated from university, he was headhunted by the Stockholm Stock Exchange and worked there for almost fifteen years, making his own fortune. He eventually returned home to Gothenburg with a wife and two kids, fulfilling a lifelong dream of having his own small business with a few high-end clients who helped build their money emporium.

Soren reestablished his relationship with Anders. Their contact over the years had been sporadic but he'd never stopped caring for his brother. It had taken some time and tweaking from Soren to be allowed back into Anders life, but eventually he'd managed to get at least a semi-stable relationship with him. The first time Luca had met Soren he'd been twelve years old, and he'd fallen for his fun and childlike uncle. He'd spent a lot of time with him and his cousins during breaks and other school holidays at their Onsala home.

Soren had quickly seen the shy little boy in Luca and taken him under his wing. He promised to never let what happened to his brother, happen to Luca. So, when Luca had finally gotten hold of his uncle and asked if he could come and spend some time with his family, Soren didn't even ask why. He simply said yes.

Luca slipped quietly out of the house later that night when everyone had gone to bed. He felt sad and slightly lost, but surprisingly not as lost as he'd felt most of this life.

It was a relief to board the shuttle, and he arrived at around midnight at Kungsbacka Station. He only had to see his uncle for his emotions to get the better of him. Luca did something he hadn't done for years; he broke down in his uncle's arms and cried. The tears slowing down to a soft sob, Soren took a step away to look at him and said, "Talk to me, Luca."

For the next hour, Luca sat in his uncle's car telling him about Kai and the past few weeks with him, all the ups and downs. He poured his heart out about his inner conflicts with his own sexuality and how he'd felt about going to med school, his parents, and, more specifically, his father. Luca said he felt betrayed by them and cheated of his life. And he was tired of feeling ashamed of his true self, but didn't know how to get rid of the shame.

At first, Soren didn't say much. He only hummed and asked a follow-up question once in a while. However, Luca could see by the look on his face when he talked about his parents that he wasn't happy. From various things Soren said, Luca could see it hurt Soren to know Anders had become similar to their father. He still felt he'd failed his younger brother, that he should have saved him from their father's claws instead of skipping town.

After Luca had gone silent, they both sat there for a moment, neither of them saying anything. Luca almost thought Soren might find a way to shove him out of the car and tell him to get lost. In his heart, Luca knew he wouldn't but the thought still occurred to him. Luca didn't dare look at his uncle as he heard him take a breath to speak.

"Luca…look at me."

He didn't look up right away, instead he closed his eyes and counted to five before he lifted his head and peered at his uncle. Luca was utterly relieved when he met the caring gaze of Soren's eyes.

"There is nothing wrong with you. Being gay is not dirty or abnormal, it's part of who you are and, to be honest, I'm not that surprised."

Luca could feel his eyes grow bigger, one of his eyebrows rising in surprise.

"Yeah, I wasn't sure of course, you never can be, but there have been small things over the years that hinted that it might be so. You never really went against their wishes on anything, but on this, you really worked hard to not let them force you to date any of the girls they tried to set you up with. In their hearts, in his heart, Luca, I think he knew, too, and that's why he fought so hard to prove himself wrong."

Luca let out a deep sigh and opened his mouth to say something but closed it again. He didn't want to sound dumb and like a perpetual child, but eventually he looked up at Soren and said, "So you don't hate me for being this way? You don't think any less of me?" Luca could hear the panic in his own voice as he waited for Soren's reply.

"Luca, for heaven's sake, of course I don't. It doesn't matter to me at all who you choose to love as long as they're good people. I couldn't care less and, honestly, Luca, most people don't care."

He stopped for a minute as if considering what he wanted to say but eventually he stated, "You told me you feel ashamed, and that you don't know how to get rid of that feeling. Do you know what I think would help?"

Luca shook his head slightly.

"I think you should start to use the word gay to describe yourself instead of all these derogatory words and labels you use. You have to stop putting yourself down and work hard on getting what you've been taught about what's expected of you out of your system. I'm not claiming it'll be easy. But only you can change your life, and choose to take a different path than the one that has been made for you. If you don't accept and love yourself for who you are, then why should others? It might be a cliché but it's true."

Luca actually smiled AND reached out to hug his uncle as best as he could in the narrow space of the car. He was so relieved he had someone on his side, who didn't want to judge him or change him, and was willing to accept him as he was—no matter if it was right or wrong.

"Thank you, Uncle Soren." Luca sniffled, throwing himself over the console again to give his uncle one last tight hug.

"Don't thank me, Luca. There's nothing to thank me for. Actually, I should be thanking you for having so much faith in me that you felt you could come to me with this." He smiled and started the car.

"Now, let's get you home, Marie has made up the guest bedroom for you. You'll get some sleep and in the morning we'll talk more if you like and figure out how to get hold of this boyfriend of yours, huh?"

That made him smile widely, and a few happy tears fell down his cheeks. At that moment, he felt the last weight lift from his chest, and for the first time believed maybe everything would be okay. They drove in silence to Soren's house; the closer they came, the more tired Luca felt. By the time they turned into his driveway, he was so exhausted he didn't know if he could make it inside. But he slowly opened the car door before Soren wrapped an arm around Luca's shoulder and walked him to the house.

Marie was at the door, holding it open as they stepped inside. She didn't ask questions or mind his late arrival. She hugged him tightly, smiled and told him to skedaddle to bed. She'd see him in the morning; he didn't argue.

As he walked up the stairs to the spare bedroom, he heard them talking. Soren filled his wife in on what was going on but Luca was too tired to even care. Marie's angry voice carried through the house as she said her piece of mind, and what she'd like to do to Luca's father next time she saw him. Luca's head hit the pillow and, as he drifted off to sleep, he heard them coming up the stairs. Soren must have calmed his wife down; Marie was still annoyed but she was no longer shouting. The last thing Luca heard was Marie telling Soren they'd have to do whatever they could to make him feel appreciated and at home. It was important to help him through this. Luca managed another smile as sleep took him under.

Bringing Hope

THE NEXT MORNING Luca didn't wake up until past ten and, by the time he actually got up, it was almost ten-thirty. At home, he was never allowed to stay in bed that long; someone would knock on his door by eight-thirty or nine at the absolute latest. But, he'd needed the sleep for sure. By the time he'd gone to bed last night, he'd been exhausted for more reasons than one. After days of worrying and dealing with the tension at home, when he'd finally gotten to a safe port, it had all caught up to him.

He felt slightly better today, but guilt was eating him up, and he felt as if he'd betrayed Kai and led him on. Luca thought about the times they'd shared the soft touches in public and how careful Kai had been not to push too much, too fast, and to not touch him "inappropriately." Now Luca wished he hadn't cared, that he'd taken every opportunity to lace his fingers with his, touch his face, look into his warm, kind eyes, and show him how much he cared; how much he loved him.

They were on their fourth day of not talking, and it was driving Luca nuts as well as scaring the life out of him. What if he was never coming back and he'd never see him again because Kai'd had enough? All because Luca had been hiding what they were to each other, and because he couldn't admit he was gay.

He got out of bed to pull on a pair of jeans and a clean T-shirt. Barefoot, Luca walked downstairs to the kitchen where Marie was.

"Morning, Luca." She smiled and kissed him on the cheek. "How are you this morning, sweetheart?"

"I'm okay. A little tired to be honest but I'm good." For some reason he felt embarrassed and looked down at his feet. He couldn't explain why, really. It was the feeling that he'd been deceiving people around him for years, exactly like he'd done to himself. Marie didn't seem to mind, but that didn't mean she wasn't upset with him. He spoke in a low voice, which almost didn't carry over the noise of the faucet she was washing her hands under.

"Marie."

She turned her head and looked at him with questioning eyes; turning the faucet off and drying her hands, she waited for Luca to continue.

"I'm sorry for lying to you. But I didn't know myself…well, I did…but I didn't." He heard himself babbling, unsure how to make himself stop. Luca felt he needed to explain himself, but how could he do that when he still didn't know how it all happened?

Before he knew it, Marie was standing in front of him, and she leaned in to cup his face. She was shorter than him, but at this moment she seemed taller and like he was the little boy who needed comfort.

"Luca, look at me."

His gaze met hers, and he couldn't see anything but love in her eyes.

"I don't care, my darling, that you're gay. What you're going through isn't easy, Luca. You're only twenty, no one expects you to have yourself all figured out." She reached up and gave him another kiss on his cheek; it made him smile.

"You're a good, young man, Luca, and considering what an asshole you have for a father, I'm even less surprised it took this long to figure things out!" She snorted and Luca tried not to laugh but it was hard to do.

"Wow. Remind me to never piss you off, Aunt Marie. Really. You're mean when you're angry."

Marie stopped what she was doing, turning to Luca with cheeks slightly pinked.

"Luca, I'm so sorry. I should never have said that to you. I didn't mean to be vulgar." She hesitated, and Luca saw she was trying to choose her next words carefully.

"It's just that your dad...he does try my patience sometimes, and it makes me angry beyond belief the way he treats you, his own flesh and blood. But I'm sorry for speaking badly about him." She stroked Luca's hair and gave him a devilish smile.

"It's okay. I sort of don't like him very much myself at the moment." Luca shrugged.

"Well, okay then. Then let me put it like this. What I'm sorry for is that I said it to your face." She smiled and gave him a wink. "Now, sit down, and I'll make your breakfast."

He tried telling her he could make something himself but, of course, she wouldn't hear of it. While she made scrambled eggs and toast, they chatted. As Marie put the plate of food and a glass of orange juice in front of Luca, she sat opposite him and gave him an intense look.

"So, Luca, tell me about this boy of yours. Kai, is it?"

Soren must have filled her in on everything the night before and, instead of feeling like they'd invaded his privacy, he felt as if they really cared and wanted to help. So, the minute she mentioned Kai's name, Luca almost bounced in his chair, eyes lighting up. As he started to tell her about this amazing cowboy in boots, his face grew hot. He wasn't used to speak so openly and freely about the man who was the recipient of his affection. As a matter of fact, besides talking to his uncle the night before about what happened, and that had been more of a confession about being gay, he hadn't talked to anyone about Kai himself.

He shuffled the eggs around his plate, smiling like a goof, his mind flashing images of his Kai. Luca's skin still tingled from the memory of his touch. His blush deepened as he remembered their one and only night together at Kai's apartment. The soft classical rock music played in the background, and only candlelight lit up the room. As the flicker of light glazed over Kai's bronzed skin, it looked like fire dancing over his body.

"He's that amazing, huh?" Marie grinned from ear to ear. "Now share, tell me about him, I want to know it all." She sipped her coffee as she waved her hand in front of Luca to get him talking.

Luca laughed at Marie's eagerness for him to share his relationship with Kai. It made him feel giddy and appreciated.

"Yeah, actually he is…he's dreamy, and a cowboy." Luca leaned his chin into his hands and watched Marie as she made a groaning sound, letting her eyes roll back and fanning her face.

"Nooo! You're kidding me, right?"

Luca shook his head and chuckled. She leaned in closer and waggled her eyebrows. "Did he wear chaps?"

The question made Luca snort; he laughed so hard, he flung his head back, mouth open to get room to breathe.

Soren walked into the kitchen and gave his wife and nephew confused looks but smiled and poured himself a coffee. "What did I miss?" He let out a chuckle as he looked at Luca who was still bent over laughing. Marie answered her husband with a big smile and a wink.

"Did you know Kai is a cowboy in chaps?" She nodded eagerly and gave her husband a wide grin. "Luca found a real live cowboy, honey. If I buy you chaps, Soren, will you wear them?"

The question made Luca laugh even harder and he almost felt sorry for Soren who nearly choked on his drink. He shook his head at her like she'd completely lost her mind, then left the room laughing quietly, mumbling about getting his neck out of a lasso.

She asked him how they'd met and if Kai was handsome. That reminded him of the picture he had, and he got it to show her. She gave him a big thumbs up and fanned herself, making Luca chuckle again. It felt nice to share that with someone who was genuinely interested, because they cared for him and wanted him to be happy. Luca poured his heart out and told Marie all the details of their first meeting. How awkward he'd been but what a gentleman Kai had turned out to be, and how they'd spent the entire day together.

Sitting there in Marie and Soren's kitchen, talking about Kai, felt like the most natural thing in the world to Luca. He told her how it felt like they'd known each other for years instead of merely hours, and how, from the moment he met Kai, he'd made him feel whole. That fact made so much more sense now than it had done that day. Luca finally understood why Kai's easygoing nature and acceptance of himself made Luca feel so light and carefree when he was with him. Kai had known all along what Luca had suppressed about himself and, in Kai, Luca's soul had found a true sense of belonging he'd hungered so long for.

He must have stopped talking because Marie's hands were touching his, and she had a deep frown between her eyes.

"Luca darling, are you all right?"

He smiled brightly at her, and nodded. Luca realized like a lightning bolt in a clear sky what he wanted and needed. The utter joy and peace he felt washing through his body made him want to stand up and scream at the top of his lungs.

"I love him, Aunt Marie!" He felt free, excited, and like he was about to burst as he said those words aloud. The chair made an awful scraping noise against the tile floor as Luca shot out of his chair.

"Yes, dear, I can see that." She tilted her head to the side and smiled at Luca as the revelation hit him straight on.

Luca felt like his mind and heart were working together for once. As the saying goes, the light went on, as he let himself feel more of the feelings he'd been denying himself for so long.

"From the look of it, Kai has been a life-changing event, Luca. I'm really proud of you. You've taken some huge steps in a very short amount of time. I really hope you'll get a chance to enjoy each other for at least a little longer; and, if you work hard at it, forever."

Luca studied her, returning her wide smile with one of his own. He'd never been so sure of anything in his life. He wanted this, he'd accepted himself and who he was completely, and he knew it was because of how he felt about Kai. All he wanted to do was tell him, and see the bright smile that would spread across his face as he told him how he felt—but he couldn't get hold of him.

Luca knew that the way he'd acted toward Kai during the past couple of months, running hot and cold, had sent mixed signals, and it had strained Kai and their relationship. He didn't blame Kai for ultimately getting to the point of no return, or at least being so upset that he'd stay away and let Luca take the first step to making things right.

However, to make things right, Kai had to be willing to talk to him, and it was as if he'd fallen off the edge of the earth. He was nowhere to be found. Luca had tried calling him many times, and gone round there, but there'd been no answer. That scared him to the point where his stomach turned into knots.

In a matter of minutes, his good mood went from an all-time-high to a nauseating low. Luca picked up his plate and glass and brought it over to the sink, rinsing it off before putting it in the dishwasher.

"Did you have a fight?" Marie appeared behind him and slid a comforting hand down his back, giving him a slight smile.

"Yes, a few days ago, I haven't been kind to him, Aunt Marie. He's given me so much, and I've only given him heartache and grief, because of all the hiding, and if I'm honest—the lies. I've lied to myself so long, and even admitting to myself that I'm…that I'm gay, has been hard. He has been so patient, but who can blame him if he's had enough." Luca's voice trailed off.

He didn't want to think about how he'd feel if Kai was gone for good. The thought of never seeing him again made his stomach tighten, and he had to swallow hard to get the lump in his throat to finally slip away. How was he going to face the world as this "new" self without Kai there with him, supporting him and showing him how to be comfortable in his own skin?

But, most of all, he couldn't stand the thought of not getting to tell Kai how much he loved him, even if it meant not hearing it back or having Kai push him away for good. Luca knew he'd never forgive himself, or ever be able to move on, if he didn't at least see Kai one last time.

He fished out his phone from his pocket, and tapped the screen to make the phone call but, like before, there was nothing.

Luca remembered meeting one of Kai's other close friends and racked his brain to remember what his name was. It was Erik! His face must have lit up like a Christmas tree when he remembered his full name was Erik Olsson. He logged on to the Internet to find his phone number and saw the new mail notification. His finger slid across the screen and he was so happy when he saw it was from Kai that it brought tears to his eyes from relief.

"Are you all right?"

"Yes, yes I'm perfect. I have an email from Kai!"

Marie had come over to put her hand on Luca's shoulder, giving it a slight squeeze. She scolded Luca teasingly for thinking Kai had dropped off from the face of the earth.

But as Luca started to read the email, his heart was beating frantically for completely other reasons. The tears in his eyes were no longer happy tears and, instead of drying up, they became heavier; within minutes, tears of heartache were rolling down Luca's cheeks.

"Luca, what on earth's the matter? What did he write?"

She didn't wait for him to answer. Instead, she took his phone from him and read what Kai had written. The more she read, the more sorrowful her features became; for Luca's sake, and a young man she'd never met.

Marie had to wipe her eyes as she put down Luca's phone on the counter. She was so touched by the open and heartfelt message from one lover to another.

Luca couldn't stop the tears from falling down his face, dripping off his chin, soaking his shirt. For heaven's sake, he was even sniffling like a little kid. He felt raw, like someone had walked in and ripped his heart out before leaving him bleeding all over the kitchen floor, letting him die a slow and painful death.

Minutes ago, he hadn't wanted to think about how it would feel to never see Kai again, to not be able to touch his face, kiss his sweet lips, or see him smile. As he stood there thinking of all the things he'd never get to see or do with Kai again, he remembered their night spent together. How amazingly beautiful Kai had been, and how Luca had trailed his sun-kissed skin with his fingers, never getting enough of touching him. That one night had been the most amazing night in Luca's life and, as he thought about not ever having it again, he slid his arms around himself as if to shelter himself from the flashing images of them being happy and in each other's arms.

"I'll never see him again, will I? I just found him, and now he's gone because I'm a coward. A stupid, pathetic coward!"

"You are not a coward or pathetic, Luca, and that email says nothing of the sort, either. So you stop that, right now!"

He looked at Marie with a tear-drenched face, feeling every ounce of pain and anger.

Initially, Marie merely stood there, obviously trying to find the right words. But then she pulled him into her arms and hugged him fiercely. "It will be all right, my darling. I know you're hurting and in such pain. I can see it in your eyes."

Luca clung to her and cried his heart out.

FINDING HOME

LUCA COULDN'T BELIEVE he was finally here. It had taken six months and some serious planning, with a lot of help from his aunt and uncle, to do this.

He watched the landscape unfold in front of him as he drove along the country road, stunned by the beauty. Even if it was November and it should be cold, it wasn't. Today, the temperature had gone up to the mid-sixties. He couldn't remember seeing anything like it before, not that at the age of twenty-one he was a seasoned traveler, but he'd been to a few places with his parents over the years. Texas was so different to the coastal city of Gothenburg—there was no comparison.

Much had happened in Luca's life since that day, six months ago, when his entire world had come tumbling down, and crushed everything he held dear.

He'd gotten Kai's email telling him he'd left without giving Luca a chance to explain or think. At that time, he hadn't had much, and Kai had been the only person who he thought fully understood him, who made him feel safe. In the first instance, Luca had been upset and had cried more than he'd ever cried in his life. After a couple of days, he'd become angry, cursing Kai for ruining his life. He'd even tried to go back on himself so to speak, and deny his feelings—what he'd done, what they'd done. Everything eventually calmed down, though, and, when it had, it was like Luca had stepped out from a thick fog and everything became crystal clear.

A plan had started to form in his head. His aunt and uncle had been there for him the entire time, helping him through the hardest time in his life. If it wasn't for their encouragement and support, he wasn't sure he'd be where he was right now. He'd thought they'd be mad but they never hesitated, telling him this was his chance to be happy, to grow as the young man he was. Both of them promised to always be there for him and helped him out with all the arrangements.

The very next day, Luca had gotten the ball rolling, taking charge of his life. Going from pleasing others to doing what made him happy. It had given him such confidence that he'd outed himself to all of his friends and most of his family.

When it came down to it, no one really minded or even raised an eyebrow. Some of his friends even said they'd already suspected or flat out knew, because they'd seen him with Kai, and there'd been no misunderstanding what they were to each other.

It had stung and made his heart ache, because it made him miss Kai even more, and he'd let him slip away. However, he kept telling himself he'd see Kai soon, and hoped he'd still be open to him. He'd had some things to take care of at home first and to sort himself out before meeting Kai again.

Luca decided that when he saw Kai, he'd meet a changed man in Luca. No matter if Kai had moved on or not, which he hoped he hadn't, Luca needed to have finished processing what being gay meant to him. He wanted to be comfortable in his own skin, and have dealt with all his demons. The worst ones were his parents, particularly his dad.

Soren and Marie had driven him back to his parents' house after living with them for almost two months. During that time, he'd only spoken to his mother a couple of times, assuring her he was doing well.

Soren had many loud discussions with his father over the phone, and even once outside their house when Luca's father had driven down to Onsala to get his son. Soren had been calm as a clam for every minute of Anders' yelling and name-calling. After he'd finished, Soren had told his younger brother to grow a backbone and go home, then he'd turned around and walked back into the house, locking the door.

Luca had wanted to confront his parents alone but his aunt and uncle wanted to be there for support; they knew what Anders' temper was like. They'd made a deal, they'd drive him up there and stay in the car. It was important to Luca that, when it came to confronting his father, he showed him he was confident and comfortable in who he was, and nothing would make him change.

Nothing of what had happened when Luca walked through the front door of his house surprised him. He'd known from the very start his father wouldn't have come to some remarkable epiphany that he'd been acting like an ass, and embrace Luca as he begged for forgiveness.

Exactly as Luca had predicted, he'd barely made it inside the door before Anders stormed out into the hallway. He'd been pointing his finger and waving his arms around, demanding an explanation from Luca, only to reel off a list of things Luca had to do if he ever wanted to redeem himself in his father's eyes. For whatever time it was that Anders spoke, Luca had only listened. There really hadn't been any point in trying to get anything in before the man had spat all his shit out.

Luca had only listened with half an ear to the barrage of words. Did Luca have any idea how incredibly embarrassing and shameful it was to walk into work and have people stare because they found out, he, Dr. Anders von Bergendahl, had a gay son?

At that point, Luca was so damn annoyed with him he pointed out they'd probably looked at him because they thought he acted like such a fucking dumbass for reacting the way he did over having a gay son. Anders hadn't said a word; instead, he'd taken the few steps separating them and slapped Luca so hard across the face he'd tumbled backward.

Anders had stood there fuming, and Luca could have sworn he would've charged him again if his mother hadn't decided for once to speak up and told Anders, "Enough!"

That had been the first time since he'd set foot through the door he'd even noticed his mother was there. As he watched her pull Anders back by the arm, he couldn't believe the woman he saw in front of him was the same person he called mother. He thought she'd changed, been willing to drop her facade, and accept him for who he was and mostly be on his side. But, as he stood there, his face throbbing, her lack of action before the assault, clearly told him, she'd only wanted to stop another disaster from happening. She might have convinced Luca on the phone she didn't mind, but she *did* mind that her son wasn't "normal."

Luca hadn't spent another moment in that house. He didn't even bother saying goodbye. He'd simply turned around and walked out the same way he'd walked in.

That had been the last time he'd talked to either of his parents. As far as he knew, his mother had made only one attempt after that to reach him—he'd never returned her call.

He'd written down a list of things he wanted from his room besides his clothes, and his uncle had gone back for Luca to retrieve them.

He let out a deep sigh and shifted in his seat, shaking his head a little as he thought of his parents. Luca still wasn't over it. The two people who created him, raised him, had turned their backs on him for the simple fact he was gay. He'd probably never be able to let all the sorrow go, knowing he'd never have a close relationship to either of his parents.

However, he did have his aunt and uncle, and they were as supportive as any parents could have been. If it weren't for them, he wouldn't be in Texas right now. He'd come a long way in six months and was proud of the person he'd become. He no longer avoided looking himself in the eyes as he stood in front of the mirror. Instead, he met his own gaze head on, and saw a confident young man who had grown from being little more than a boy in some ways to actually being a man. The type of man he wanted to be for himself, and who he wanted Kai to meet.

He was getting closer now—according to the GPS in his rental car, he was only about half a mile away. His heart started to beat faster as he thought that, in a few minutes, he'd be driving up to Kai's family farm and he had no idea how Kai would react.

Luca never did email Kai back or call him. So many times, he'd picked the phone up or started an email he later deleted.

After Luca had taken the time he felt he needed to sort himself out, he'd looked up Kai's friend Erik and told him everything. Erik had given him Kit's phone number, Kai's older brother. He'd been so nervous when he actually picked up the phone to call Kit that he almost hung up on him as Kit said hello. He laughed at himself, remembering Kit saying hello about four times before Luca blurted out who he was.

Kit had gone very quiet, then he'd said, "I've heard about you, Luca. You broke my brother's heart."

Luca had felt his face burn hot as he blushed and apologized.

"Yes, I know, and I'm so sorry. I know what I did was wrong. That I was a coward, and I turned my back on him when he was the only one who stood up for me. Please, don't hate me!"

Kit had only chuckled and reassured him no one was hating anyone, least of all Kai. They'd talked for a long time, and over the months they'd kept in contact. When Luca told Kit his plan and asked if it would be okay for him to come out to see Kai at their farm, he didn't hesitate to say yes. Kit agreed, after much convincing, not to tell Kai he was coming; he couldn't quite explain it but he wanted it to be a surprise.

Luca turned into the driveway leading down to the Kelly Cattle Ranch. He realized he didn't want Kai to know because no matter what Kai's reaction was, Luca was here because he wanted to be and not purely because of Kai.

He still didn't know if Kai had moved on or not. He'd asked Kit not to tell him because the reason he was there was to apologize. If fate was on his side, he might still be able to convince Kai to give him a second chance.

As he came closer to the main house and the barns, he saw a man, not much older than himself, standing in the yard, presumably waiting for him. He'd called Kit as he left College Station, and Kit said he'd be waiting. Luca parked next to two trucks by the side of one of the barns, watching the man approach him with a smile on his face.

For a minute, he sat there trying to swallow down the lump that had grown in his throat, and dry his now very sweaty palms against his denim-covered thighs. He jumped a little as a face, looking very much like Kai's, appeared at the side window, giving him a grand smile as he waved a little. Luca couldn't help laughing and opened the door to step out. He held out his hand to the man in front of him.

"You have to be Kit. It's very nice to finally meet you. I'm Luca."

Kit shook his hand as he kept smiling at Luca, giving his shoulder a squeeze.

"How was the trip?"

"Long, and I'm jetlagged to hell."

Kit laughed and slapped Luca on the shoulder before turning around and guiding him toward the back of the house.

"It's great to finally meet you, too, Luca. You can leave your stuff in your car for now. I'll take care of it later. I'm sure you're eager to see Kai. I haven't told him you're coming, like we agreed on. But I had to tell Ma and Pops, they'd never have forgiven me otherwise." He chuckled as he pointed toward the main house and the two people who came down the stairs to greet him.

He didn't have time to prepare himself for the greeting he got from their mother. She came up, kissing and hugging him like he was an old family friend. Kai's father shook his hand and called him "son"—he couldn't have gotten a better welcome. As they chatted, and Kai's mother asked Luca all kinds of questions he tried to answer, Kai came walking out of the barn.

"Whose car was that I saw coming down the driveway?" Kai stopped walking the minute he looked up and saw Luca standing with his parents and brother.

Luca could only imagine what was going through Kai's mind as their eyes met. He felt like he wanted to reach up and rub his eyes, to make sure what he saw was actually real. His Kai, even more beautiful and studly than before, back in his natural habitat, and wearing a cowboy hat. *It was what had been missing all along*, Luca thought. His smile grew wider at the sight of his very own cowboy. Kai's eyes seemed to be saying, how could this be? It couldn't be Luca but someone who looked exactly like him. All he could hope for was that it was a good thing, him being there.

"Kai…" He took a couple of hesitant steps forward, he was still nervous, but the plain sight of Kai had him so happy he'd forgotten everyone else around him. Luca took another few steps toward him, feeling a little more secure, so that he was standing within arm's reach of Kai, but without touching him.

"Kai…" he said again, no other words escaping his lips. His mouth curved up into a smile as their eyes met in an intense stare. Luca could see the flicker of joy and confusion, and even fright, as it flashed in Kai's eyes. He wanted to say more but all he could think about was how his hands itched to touch his face, his lips, run his fingers through his sun-bleached hair. He was finally home, because this was where his heart was, on a ranch in Texas, with his cowboy.

"Luca. What are you doing here?" Kai smiled as he kept watching Luca; he must've been able see how happy Luca was to see him, but for once, it was Kai holding back, not Luca. His eyes flitted back to his parents and to Kit, whose expressions made it clear that Luca being here was no surprise. Kai's reaction so far, or lack of, gave Luca hope— hope that he wasn't going to kick him off his land and say he never wanted to see him again.

Kai's eyes returned to his, golden brown and full of welcoming warmth. Both men looked at each other, studying, searching, waiting for the other one to finally say something.

Luca's strength had never been to shield his emotions, and he hoped when Kai looked into his eyes now, he'd see all the old insecurities he'd had were mostly gone.

"Luca, what are you doing here?" Kai repeated, stumbling over some of his words.

"I'm sorry…I'm so happy to see you. You look good, Kai, being home suits you."

184

Kai didn't give a response but stood there looking at him. He seemed rather nervous, actually, and the fact he was nervous made Luca realize this was his chance to take charge, to show Kai he was a changed man.

So, he took the last step toward Kai, invading his space, but he didn't care. He reached down between them and took Kai's hand in his. When he didn't pull away, he intertwined his fingers with Kai's before looking up and meeting his eyes.

"I came out to my parents, my aunt and uncle, my friends...to everyone, Kai. I had more or less decided before I saw your email, but you leaving gave me that final push I needed to see what you'd seen all along." He took a deep breath, never letting his eyes wander but looking steadily at Kai.

Kai's eyebrows shot up. "You did? Really? What happened? What did your parents say? Are you okay?" Kai's free hand came up to squeeze his shoulder, and Luca could see he was uneasy asking the question, like he suspected something had gone badly wrong.

"My parents, especially my father, had an outburst that would take a good week to describe so I'll spare you the details. But let's just say that he hit me in the face and pretty much ended my relationship with him."

Kai's hand tensed in his and Luca squeezed it reassuringly. Reaching up, he cupped Kai's cheek, letting out a deep, happy sigh that sounded like he hadn't taken a deep, healing breath in a very long time.

"It's okay." He smiled broadly to show Kai he meant it, and let his thumb brush over his cheek softly. "My aunt and uncle, and actually most of my friends, have been very supportive. I'm sorry I didn't call or write to you, but I felt it was important that for us to work, I needed to figure things out on my own, for me, you know. I wanted to come and see you, being confident, sure, and happy in myself, not confused. You deserve that much." He could hear himself babbling, but he couldn't help it.

"I've missed you so much. I missed you every minute of every day, the way you look at me, the way your voice sounds, I've missed your strength, and most of all I've missed talking to you, seeing your face." Luca took a deep breath.

"I love you, Kai Kelly, and I hope you'll give me…us, a second chance. I'm so sorry I pushed you away." He finally fell silent. He'd said everything he'd come to say, the ball was in Kai's court now.

Kai's didn't say anything and that made Luca nervous. What if he was trying to figure out how to let him down gently?

Then, as suddenly as Kai had appeared from the barn, Luca was swept into his arms, and Kai was hugging him tightly, his lips right by Luca's ear as he whispered, "I've dreamed of this. I've dreamed of hearing you say that, of you being ready to be who you are with no shame."

He leaned back, staring into Luca's eyes with a massive smile on his face, his eyes shining. He cupped Luca's face, stroking his now quite long hair out of the way. "You let your hair grow out. It looks good on you, all you need now is a cowboy hat and you'll fit right in." He chuckled.

Kai slid his arm around Luca's shoulder, pulling him in even closer to nuzzle the side of his face, the familiar scent that was Kai right there in his nose was so good, it almost made him high. Their eyes met, and Kai's eyes flickered down to Luca's lips as his tongue swept out to run over his dry lips in anticipation. Kai leaned in and brushed his lips over Luca's, first gently before they latched on to each other like their lives depended on it. The kiss deepened, tongues flicking out, tasting, teeth scraping against skin and clinking together.

It was intoxicating feeling Kai this close to him again, his taste and his scent everywhere, being out in the open, loving him for the world to see even if that world was only three people. He wrapped his arms around Kai's waist, running his hands up and down his back. How could he have forgotten how wonderful Kai tasted, and how soft his lips were, kissing him gave him the feeling of being home.

It was Kai who broke off the kiss and, as they both breathed hard, trying to gather their breaths, Kai leaned his forehead against Luca's. "I still can't believe you're here, and the man who stands here, kissing me in the open of my parents' ranch for anyone to see, is not the shy Luca I left in Gothenburg six months ago." He grinned and pecked Luca on the lips once more.

"No. I sent him packing."

Kai threw his head back, laughing hard. Luca watched him beaming, so happy his Kai was overjoyed to see him.

"Not all of him, I hope. I sort of liked that shy, sweet guy," Kai said between laughs.

"No, not all of him, his essence is still here." Luca made a face. "Can I stop talking about myself in third person now?"

Kai laughed some more. "You sure can. How long are you here, Luca?"

"For as long as you want me. I've enrolled at Texas A & M. I'll be starting vet school in January."

Kai's eyes lit up with enough sparkle to power the City of Gothenburg.

That was when Luca couldn't hold his laughter back anymore, his head fell back and he felt like screaming to the sky how happy he was he wouldn't be going home anytime soon. He didn't know what would happen, but that was okay. Right now, right here, all he wanted in life, he had.

He was going to vet school, something he'd dreamed about since he was a boy, and he was doing it in a part of the world he'd always wanted to explore, with someone he loved. Nothing else mattered.

Kai gave him a funny look and laughed quietly at Luca's exuberance.

Kai's mother appeared on the porch and smiled at them. "Are you boys ready for some lunch?"

Kai took his hand slowly but surely, leading Luca toward the house. As they walked, Luca told Kai about Texas A & M, vet school, and his full scholarship. The more Luca told him about his five-year-plan, the broader Kai's grin became. It told Luca the feeling he had of finally finding home was right. Kai smiled at him.

"What?" Luca smiled back. "Do I have dirt on my face?" he joked, nudging Kai's side as they walked.

"No. You're perfect, baby. Just perfect!" Smiling widely, with his arm secured tightly around Luca's waist, Kai leaned in and kissed his temple as he whispered into his ear, "Welcome home!"

ABOUT THE AUTHOR

Phetra H. Novak

Phetra often refers to herself as the odd man out, the dorky book nerd. She'd rather spend time with a good book or making up fantastic stories with even more fantastic characters, than live in the real world, dealing with real people.

The real world is strange, in a very non-humorous way, and people in it complicate it to the point of wearing you out. In the written word world, whether it's someone else's words or her own, things might get busy, complicated, and even downright painful, but somewhere along the line, a hero's always on the horizon. He's probably not a prim and proper, church-going pretty-boy since the author prefers rebellious men and women who don't follow the protocols of society.

One of her favorite sayings is that "Only dead fish follow the stream," and well she ain't no dead fish.

Phetra lives with her family—two children, a domestic partner, and their two cats in Gothenburg, Sweden. When reading her books, you'll notice she always finds a way to bring her own culture into her stories.

The joy of reading and writing comes from her childhood and is something she has always loved, and been passionate to share with others. Phetra loves hearing from her readers, even with ideas of what they'd like to come next.

If you are looking for her, the best place to start looking is at home in the quietest corner of the house, where she'll be curled up with either her Kindle, reading or with her laptop typing away.

You can contact Phetra on: http://www.phetranovak.com/

By the Author

Out Now…

**If you enjoyed this story, look out for the
Caddo Norse series.**

FATED FUTURE

**Available now for FREE on Amazon and All
Romance**

A Caddo Norse Novelette: 0.5

1964. Vojin Naranjo is a young Caddo man in his small
workshop, together with his best friend Gabriel working.
What he doesn't know is that the man who he's known all
his life isn't who he's said he is. Gabriel carries a secret, one
that no one knows nothing about but that Vojin now is to
take part of. There's only one catch no matter what Vojin
can't share it with anyone or if he does he will seal a deadly
fate for everyone involved. The question is how will Vojin
Naranjo react to the news of what fate has already decided
for his unborn son and grandson? How will he prepare
himself to save those he loves?

1992. Years later, in another part of the country, the Asa
Guards are preparing for war, with their Gods leading the

way. The cunning Asa are using the little more than human Guards as their willing-to-die soldiers in the war against the Fenrir Ulv and his newborn children, the shifters. The man leading the Guard, Colonel Gustav sells his soul to the God of the sky, Odin in a hope of spending eternal next to the mighty God. Will the Guard follow him or desert him?

2009. Haven is having his twenty-first birthday, Reid and the other ranch hands have taken him to Tom's bar in town. There he is, at his dismay, propositioned by the town skank, Mrs. Harris. Giving the woman's very touchy-feely nature, he finally gives her a piece of his mind, leaving her with her mouth hanging open and he himself is pissed off. Back at the ranch, he goes to see Bullet, a white and brown mottled horse, and his birthday present from his friends. Looking for peace he's instead confronted by the eighteen-year-old Alexander. Already riled up and riding his emotion Haven let himself get carried away in a heated moment with the boy of his heart's desire. What will Alexander and Haven do when the moment is gone and reality comes crashing down?

Genre: LGBTQ, M/M, Paranormal, Norse Mythology, Caddo Native, sensual erotic romance.

HAVEN'S REVENGE

Available now on Amazon and All Romance

A Caddo Norse Novel: Book One

Haven Naranjo is a proud Caddo Indian, with a frightening past. He was a mere fifteen-year-old boy when he found his parents, part of his tribe, and his high school sweetheart slaughtered by a wereman gone mad. Falling victim to a system that is not always prepared to deal with a shattered young mind, Haven finally gives up on himself. He grows up to be bitter and hateful toward the creatures he hates. Werewolves.

Alexander Prescott is the younger of the two Prescott boys and comes from a large werewolf clan. But things are bigger than that. Alexander, is the true vessel of the Fenrir Ulv and is to become the leader of all supernatural beings, the King of Wolves. On top of that, he's in love with Haven. He's known since he hit puberty that Haven is his true mate. But there's one problem, Haven hates what he can become. However, Alexander has a plan on how he is to charm his, and his wolf's way into the grumpy Caddo Indian man's heart.

But fate has other plans for them. The Asa Guard enters their calm country living, determined to use their own kind against them and kill the true vessel—Alexander Prescott.

When war between the Asa Gods and the Fenrir Ulv starts knocking on their door, what side will the damaged Haven choose? Will he find a way of trusting those, especially

Alexander, who he feels has betrayed him and let his animal, the eagle, lead him straight to his fate by his mate's side? Or will he trust the words of strangers, who come to make his quest of seeing all shifters dead a reality?

Haven's Revenge is a story of an emotional journey for a whole community. It's about finding acceptance, not just from others but in yourself.

Coming Soon...

Other titles releasing soon from this author:

LOVE OF THE GAME

Coming 2016

The Love of Series: Book One

Johannes, a young man, is starting his new life as a rookie in the best hockey league in the world, the NHL. His new home for the next four years in Montreal, Canada has him excited to get to his destination when a storm arrives, stranding him in Charlies de Gaulle Airport in Paris, France.

He's been standing by the VIP bar trying to amuse himself the best he can, and nursing a lukewarm beer. He's about to head back to his company when the most gorgeous man he's ever seen, with piercing green eyes, bumps into him. He swears he has never been so instantly turned on as he is in that moment. The man flirts openly with him, making no secret of what he wants from Johannes as he invites him to meet in the men's room. Not being out only makes Johannes hesitate for a moment before accepting the beautiful stranger's come-on.

Charlie, a cocky and opinionated, ex submissive, reporter is leaving Paris after being on vacation when the studly jock just happens to appear out of nowhere—served on a silver platter. Charlie sees no reason to deny himself a last rendezvous before he gets on his plane back to Canada.

What he doesn't expect is this stranger to see the real him. Charlie's normal plan of attack is to take charge. But when it backfires, and the studly stranger not only takes control but makes him want more, Charlie does the only thing he feel comfortable doing. He runs!

SILENT TERRORISM

Coming 2016

Terrorism Series: Book One

Ebbe Skoog, a Swedish correspondent camera man is stationed in Saudi Arabia with his colleague and best friend, sometimes fuck buddy, Mattis Andersson. He is out early one morning, shooting with his camera for an upcoming piece he and Mattis are working on, when he stumbles on something he shouldn't see. On a building site, right outside the city of Riyadh, four men looking awfully like the Mutawa, the religious police, are on their way to sending a bound man to a certain death by stoning.

With his camera still rolling, Ebbe gets it all on film, and is just starting to think about retreating when a new man enters the scene. Throwing himself on top of the now dying man to save him, he sobs for his lover not to leave him. Being a gay man himself, Ebbe reacts before his logic can stop him and in a whirlwind of emotions, he steps out of his hiding place. With his camera in one hand, he more or less carries the screaming lover out of the oncoming rain of stones.

They manage to flee the scene but they're only out of immediate danger. It won't stay that way for long.

While Ebbe flees across the Middle Eastern desert to save himself, his companion Aasim El-Batal, and the chip containing the horrible footage that will make Saudi Arabia burn in the eyes of human rights activist all over the world.

Ebbe's partner, Mattis Andersson, the wild card and the rebel of the two is the only man left standing. Fighting to get his friend and the death sentenced man out.

Both men are now wanted by not only the Saudi government who wants to see the shameful, sick animals taken out but the Swedish government wants them out of the country and silenced, too. They can't jeopardize years of working relationships and weapons deals with the Saudi's for some petty gay love affair. And as for the Swedish Prime Minister, he's more concerned about the aching need between his legs than the aching need of his countrymen for a fierce and righteous leader.